"I saw you making eye...

sai...
ne...
go...

wl...
Jo...

Ni...

wi...
ou...
no...
ali...
ris...

yc...
kn...
bu...
tre...

wa...
he...
fr...

E...
tw...
w...

SWEET VALLEY HIGH™

Don't dare miss these extra-long special editions of the top-selling teenage series, Sweet Valley High – now on TV too!

The Sweet Valley High series is published by Bantam Books.

SWEET VALLEY High®

ELIZABETH'S RIVAL

Written by
Kate William

Created by
FRANCINE PASCAL

BANTAM BOOKS
NEW YORK · TORONTO · LONDON · SYDNEY · AUCKLAND

ELIZABETH'S RIVAL
A BANTAM BOOK : 0 553 50445 2

Originally published in USA by Bantam Books

First publication in Great Britain

PRINTING HISTORY
Bantam edition published 1996

The trademarks "Sweet Valley" and "Sweet Valley High"
are owned by Francine Pascal and are used under license by
Bantam Books and Transworld Publishers Ltd.

Conceived by Francine Pascal

Produced by Daniel Weiss Associates, Inc,
33 West 17th Street, New York, NY 10011

Cover photo by Oliver Hunter

Bantam Books are published by Transworld Publishers Ltd,
61–63 Uxbridge Road, Ealing, London W5 5SA,
in Australia by Transworld Publishers (Australia) Pty Ltd,
15–25 Helles Avenue, Moorebank, NSW 2170,
and in New Zealand by Transworld Publishers (NZ) Ltd,
3 William Pickering Drive, Albany, Auckland.

Printed and bound in Great Britain by
Cox & Wyman Ltd, Reading, Berkshire.

To William "Billy" Anastasi

Chapter 1

"Hello, hello! I'm home!" sixteen-year-old Jessica Wakefield called out as she burst through her front door. She dropped a pile of shopping bags onto the floor and cocked her head to listen for any signs of life in the house.

Jessica heard the voice of her identical twin sister, Elizabeth, from the kitchen. ". . . I can't wait to see you again, either," Elizabeth was saying. "This is going to be the best summer ever!"

Jessica entered the kitchen just as Elizabeth was hanging up the phone. "Liz! I'm so glad you're home," Jessica gushed. "You won't believe what I found at the mall this afternoon."

"Oh, Jess!" Elizabeth spun around, raising her hand to her mouth in surprise. "Don't sneak up on me like that." Then she smiled. "But I'm glad you're here. You'll never guess who was just on the

1

phone," she said breathlessly, her blue-green eyes sparkling with excitement.

"In a minute," Jessica said. "First you have to see the cute hiking boots I found at the mall!"

Elizabeth chuckled and reached into the cupboard for a glass. "Did I hear Jessica Wakefield use the words 'cute' and 'hiking boots' in the same sentence? What happened to 'hiking boots are the biggest insult to femininity since the basketball shoe fad'?" Elizabeth asked as she poured herself some orange juice.

"All right, I deserve that," Jessica admitted, remembering how much she had griped that morning about her daunting shopping challenge ahead. "But that was before I found these. Don't move— I'll go get them." Jessica dashed out of the kitchen.

Rummaging through the pile of bags in the front hall, Jessica remembered why she had ventured out on her mission to find a wearable pair of hiking boots. She and Elizabeth were scheduled to spend the next month in the mountains of Montana, as junior counselors at a performing arts summer camp called Camp Echo Mountain. Lots of famous movie stars, writers, singers, and dancers had gone to the camp as children—which made the idea of spending a month in mosquito-infested Montana much more attractive to Jessica. *I'm sure to be discovered this summer,* Jessica fantasized as she walked back into the kitchen.

Jessica plopped her boots right on top of the kitchen table and dropped the empty shoe box beside them. "Aren't they majestic?" she said admiringly.

"They *are* nice," Elizabeth agreed, putting the boots back into their box. Her eyes fell on the other bags Jessica held in her hands. "I see that you didn't find it necessary to stop with one pair of boots."

"Well, when the first decent pair of hiking boots ever created fell into my lap, I knew today wasn't just a regular kind of day." She paused for effect and then began pulling items from the bags—colorful tank tops, sundresses, and sandals. "Look at this haul," Jessica enthused. "The planets must have been in perfect alignment."

Elizabeth stifled a giggle.

"Don't laugh," Jessica said crossly. "There are only a few truly great shopping days a year. It's a shame to waste them."

"Yeah, whatever," Elizabeth said, laughing. Shopping was a passion that the twins didn't share. Actually that was only one of many characteristics that divided the physically identical twins. The girls had the same bright blue-green eyes and slim, athletic figures, and they even shared an identical dimple in their left cheeks. But their different personalities were immediately obvious from the way they wore their good looks.

For instance, even though Jessica and Elizabeth

3

were blessed with classic California silky long blond hair, Elizabeth usually wore hers modestly pulled back in a barrette or ponytail while Jessica preferred to keep her hair loose and carefree. And while Elizabeth was a stylish dresser, her taste ran toward the more conservative looks of the day. Jessica, on the other hand, gravitated toward the boldest fashion trends.

The twins' different personalities also divided their lifestyles. Jessica was the co-captain of the cheerleading squad; Elizabeth worked on the school paper. Jessica ran around with the most popular girls at Sweet Valley High; Elizabeth enjoyed socializing on a more personal level, usually with her best friend, Enid Rollins, and her long-time boyfriend, Todd Wilkins. Jessica dreamed of being a movie star; Elizabeth dreamed of being a writer.

And Jessica lived for the moment, often throwing caution to the wind, while Elizabeth rarely acted without first considering the consequences.

But for all their contrasts, Elizabeth and Jessica were as close as only identical twins could be.

Elizabeth poured another glass of orange juice and handed it to Jessica. "So now that you've shared your big shopping news flash, are you going to let me tell you about my phone call?" she asked, feigning annoyance.

Jessica took a sip of juice. "Well, are you going

to tell me, or are you going to make me guess?"

Elizabeth crossed her arms in front of her chest. "I'd like to hear you try to guess."

"Hmmm . . . Let's see." Jessica squinted with concentration. "Why is this going to be Elizabeth's best summer ever?" She opened her eyes wide. "Did the California State Lottery Board call to say you'd won ten million dollars?"

Elizabeth rolled her eyes.

Jessica laughed. "No, Elizabeth Wakefield would never throw her money away on something so frivolous as a lottery ticket." Jessica put her finger to her lips. "Hmmm . . . did the Prince of Wales call to invite you to his palace for the summer? No, no . . . his ears are too big."

"Jess, stop it," Elizabeth said, laughing. "Those are the most pitiful guesses I've ever heard. Just give it up."

"OK. I'm stumped," Jessica admitted, sitting down at the kitchen table. "Who was it?"

Elizabeth sat down across from Jessica. "Remember my good friend Maria from junior high? Maria Slater?"

"Of course!" Jessica exclaimed. "In case you've forgotten, Liz, I was friends with Maria even before you were."

"Oh, *right*," Elizabeth said, smirking. "After you saw her in a commercial on TV, you wanted to be her best friend because you thought she would be your ticket to a successful acting career."

Jessica's mouth dropped open. "That's not the only reason!" she said, sitting straight up in her chair. "I really liked her."

"Maybe so, but you didn't like the fact that she had come to Sweet Valley to get away from Hollywood," Elizabeth pointed out. "Especially when you found out that Maria wanted to be a writer, not an actress."

"I just thought she was throwing away a promising career," Jessica maintained. But deep down she had to admit that Elizabeth was right—at least partially. Jessica couldn't believe it when she learned that Maria Slater, successful child actor, had become fed up with show business when she hit puberty and the roles stopped coming. Maria had decided to take a break from the frustrations of her stalled career by moving to Sweet Valley to stay with her sister, where she would try to live the life of a normal twelve-year-old girl in middle school.

How could anyone *not want to be a movie star?* Jessica had wondered. Before long it became clear that Elizabeth and Maria had more in common. The two of them were close friends until Maria's mother, who was a music business executive, got a great job offer with a record company in New York City and Maria moved across the country with her parents.

Elizabeth's blue-green eyes sparkled with excitement. "Anyway, Mrs. Slater's music company relocated to a corporate park just outside Sweet Valley, so the family is moving back here!" she gushed.

"That's terrific!" Jessica said enthusiastically. "But what does that have to do with this summer? We're going to be in Montana."

"That's the best part!" Elizabeth cried. "Maria's also going to be a JC at Camp Echo Mountain! With all her acting experience, she's been assigned to assist the director." Elizabeth grinned. "Maria didn't say anything, but I'm sure she'll want me to write the camp play."

Jessica gave her sister a friendly pat on the arm. "And she couldn't find a better playwright."

"Thanks, Jess," Elizabeth said warmly. "And another thing—Maria's best friend from New York is going to be a JC, too. Maria thinks we'll get along great."

Jessica frowned. She wasn't altogether happy about this development. *Between Maria and her friend, writing the play, and all our camp responsibilities, Liz won't have any time for me*, Jessica thought. "Oh, joy, the Three Musketeers," she said sarcastically.

Jessica had been looking forward to spending a lot of time with her sister this summer. Elizabeth's boyfriend, Todd, wasn't going to be hanging around her all the time—for once. And Jessica's

7

best friend, Lila Fowler—who Jessica had managed to talk into being a JC, too—had a way of getting distracted by guys. *I'm not in any mood for romance this summer,* Jessica thought. *I've been through enough trauma recently.*

Jessica's eyes welled up with tears as memories washed over her. A few months back she had taken up surfing in order to enter a local surfing contest. On her first day out Jessica met a gorgeous surfer named Christian, who agreed to be her coach. Their flirtatious friendship soured Jessica's relationship with her boyfriend, Ken Matthews. In fact, Ken and Jessica soon broke up.

Then Jessica's budding new relationship took a tragic turn when Christian was killed in a freak accident. *Christian may have been the man who would have made me happy for the rest of my life,* Jessica thought. *But I'll never know.* She wiped away a tear, cursing the strange ways of fate.

But Elizabeth didn't seem to notice her sister's distress. "Supposedly Maria's friend is a writer, too," she said now.

Jessica raised an eyebrow. "*Another* writer? Since when did writing become such a popular activity? And why didn't anyone tell me?" she asked. If writing came as naturally to Elizabeth as breathing, it came as naturally to Jessica as getting a tooth pulled.

Elizabeth went to the sink to rinse out her

8

glass. "Oh, Jess, writing isn't for everyone. Besides, I think you're a lot better at writing than you think." Then Elizabeth bounded out of the kitchen.

Jessica frowned as she scooped up her shopping bags from the floor. *Either Liz didn't notice—or didn't care—that I might feel left out,* Jessica thought. *Usually Elizabeth can tell exactly what I'm feeling and thinking. I just hope she gets back to normal before we go to Montana.*

"What do you *mean* you want to forget about guys this summer?" Lila Fowler asked Jessica incredulously. Jessica had come over to Fowler Crest that evening to help Lila pack. Lila stopped rummaging through her drawers and plopped down next to Jessica, who was sitting on Lila's queen-size bed, polishing her nails.

Jessica put down the nail buffer and turned to face Lila. "Exactly what I said," she replied. "Jessica Wakefield is going to have a boy-free summer. I just don't think I'll be in the mood to chase guys."

Lila shook her head. *Christian's death must have really wounded her,* Lila figured, watching as Jessica buffed her nails with increasing fervor. Lila had seen Jessica go through a number of phases where guys were concerned. Usually the shifts of mood meant that Jessica had decided to date one

9

boy exclusively instead of two or more at once, or older boys versus younger boys, foreign boys versus domestic, common folk versus royalty. This no-boy phase was a phase Lila had never seen before. And she didn't like it. "The best way to get over one guy is to find another," Lila said out loud.

Jessica bit her lip. "This isn't about Chri—" Jessica interrupted herself and took a deep breath. "I think this summer will be a good opportunity for us to do all the girl stuff we like to do."

"But most of the girl stuff we like to do involves guys," Lila protested.

"Well, maybe it shouldn't," Jessica grumbled, her voice catching in her throat.

Lila groaned. *The last thing I need right now is a bawling Jessica Wakefield to add to the stress of packing,* she realized. *After all, Jessica is sure to get over this phase, too.*

So she changed the subject to more a immediate matter—clothing. "Do you think there are any dry cleaners in Montana who know what they're doing?" Lila asked as she jumped up to pack a shimmery blue silk suit into her Louis Vuitton suitcase. "I hate to think this suit will have to go all month without a proper cleaning."

"I don't know, Li," Jessica said, chuckling. "Maybe you shouldn't risk it." She stood up and pulled the suit back out of the bag. "And while you're at it, better leave this at home, too," Jessica

10

added, grabbing a beaded black evening gown from under a pile of velour towels.

Lila gasped. She *loved* that dress! "But that's so unforgettable, I can't wear it more than once, anyway. I'll just send it back here to be cleaned," Lila reasoned.

Jessica shook her head. "I can't imagine why you'd wear it even once," she said, hanging the shimmery dress back up in Lila's closet. "You don't seem to be catching on to the idea of *camp*, Lila."

"But it's *performing arts* camp," Lila argued. "We'll have cast parties and opening nights."

Jessica grinned. "It won't be like going to the opera," she told her best friend. "Most of the time we'll be hiking, swimming, sailing, and pretty much roughing it." She went back to Lila's suitcase and pulled out not one but two sets of steam curlers—large for loose waves and small for tight curls—and walked with them into Lila's private bathroom.

Lila followed Jessica into the bathroom. "Since when did you become the expert on roughing it, Miss Fashion Police?"

"Since I had to use my wits to survive a desert storm, as a matter of fact," Jessica replied.

Lila opened her mouth, then closed it. She had to admit that Jessica had a point. Lila pulled her eight-step facial care system out of her cosmetic bag as she remembered the story of Jessica's horrific experience in Death Valley.

A few months back Jessica, Elizabeth, and four other students from Sweet Valley High went on what was supposed to be a week-long survival adventure trip in Death Valley. When they discovered gold, they greedily pursued more, ending up miles out of their way. They missed their pickup and had to tough out a brutal rainstorm without food or water. Then they were kidnapped by escaped convicts. Lila shuddered at the thought.

Of course, Lila wouldn't have gotten herself into that predicament. A few measly gold nuggets would never have driven her to such irresponsible greed. She had *stacks* of gold bricks in her trust fund. Still, Lila's idea of roughing it was staying in a one-star motel instead of a four- or five-star hotel.

Now Lila watched forlornly as Jessica went to the back of Lila's closet and pulled out khakis, jeans, and T-shirts and threw them into her suitcase. "Didn't you say you had hiking boots stashed away somewhere?" Jessica asked.

Lila wrinkled her nose in distaste. "I think they're way in the back . . . in a box underneath that softball mitt I never use."

"I told you that you should have bought a pair like I got today," Jessica said as she disappeared into the depths of Lila's closet. "I'm not going to even mind wearing them, they're so cute."

Lila tuned out Jessica's cheerful description of

all the wonderful outfits she could build on top of her new hiking boots. *I didn't even want to go to this stupid Camp Echo Mountain in the first place,* Lila complained silently. *Jessica better appreciate what a good friend I'm being.* The only thing that reassured Lila she wouldn't be miserable all summer long was the thought of meeting cute, creative guys from all over the country.

With a sigh, Lila thought of Robbie Goodman. Before Robbie, Lila had always rejected artsy types as being flaky and poor. But Robbie changed her mind. He *was* an artist, but he was also from a rich, cultured family. Ever since Robbie had moved away to go to art school, Lila had been yearning for another romance with an artist.

So what if Jessica wants to throw away the opportunity for romance this summer? She can't expect me to be a nun, too, Lila decided. With Jessica still crouched on the floor in the back of Lila's closet, Lila took the opportunity to pull a gold lamé bikini from her dresser, hiding it in a pocket of her suitcase.

As Daddy always says, a Fowler should be prepared for any situation, Lila thought. *And you never know when the situation calls for you to be sexy.*

"By this time tomorrow I'll be sitting with Maria Slater, catching up on all the things that have happened in the years we've been apart,"

Elizabeth gushed as Todd pulled his black BMW into a parking space. The couple had decided to spend their last night together at Miller's Point, their favorite place to be alone.

"Uh-huh," Todd grunted.

"I've always felt like something's been missing from my life since she moved away," Elizabeth continued in a pensive tone, gazing out of the car's windshield at the night sky.

"I'm sorry I couldn't be more like Maria," Todd said in a flat voice.

Elizabeth looked at her boyfriend, sucking in a gasp when she saw the hurt expression on his face. All of a sudden she heard how her last words must have sounded to Todd—like he wasn't enough to satisfy her. "Oh, Todd, I didn't mean it like that," she said, uncurling his fingers from their tight grasp on the steering wheel. She took his right hand into both of hers. "I wouldn't want you to be any different than you are. It's just that Maria and I shared a real bond—about writing. She's the only other person I've known who's as passionate about writing as I am."

Todd frowned and pulled back his hand. "I still don't know why you can't stop talking about Maria suddenly when in all the time we've gone out, you've barely mentioned her."

Todd's words stung Elizabeth. It didn't *feel* like she had forgotten about Maria or ever stopped missing her. Just because she didn't talk about Maria all the time didn't mean that Elizabeth had stopped caring a great deal about her. Or that Todd should be so cynical about their friendship.

But this was Elizabeth's last night with Todd—she didn't want to fight. She took Todd's hand again. "Let's stop talking about Maria and talk about how much I'll miss you."

"Will you miss me?" Todd asked softly.

"Of course I will," Elizabeth answered firmly, her blue-green eyes sparkling with affection. "How could I not when we'll be apart a whole month?"

"Don't remind me," Todd grumbled. "One month of you frolicking in the mountains with a bunch of gorgeous actors and writers while I'm stuck in smoggy L.A. with a bunch of sweaty guys competing on the basketball court." While Jessica and Elizabeth were at Camp Echo Mountain, Todd was going to basketball camp. The basketball camp was very elite—only the top high school basketball players in the state had been invited to go. The assistant coach of the L.A. Lakers was going to be teaching there, along with some of the top college basketball coaches in southern California.

Elizabeth looked at her boyfriend's pouty profile, which looked especially sullen in the moonlight. *First he was jealous of Maria and now he's jealous of nameless guys,* Elizabeth realized. While part of Elizabeth liked the feeling of Todd's possessiveness, the other part wished he had as much faith in their relationship as she did. "Todd, I'm surprised at you," Elizabeth said out loud, trying not to sound as annoyed as she felt. "What happened to 'The most valuable summer I could ever have hoped for'?" she asked, mimicking Todd's voice.

"It became a lot less valuable after I found out what you'll be doing," Todd grumbled.

Now Elizabeth could no longer contain her annoyance. "Todd, I'm going to pretend that you just said how happy you are that while you're off playing basketball, I'm going to have a fun summer, too." She glared at him.

Todd gulped and looked into his lap. Then he looked up and met Elizabeth's gaze. "You're right, Liz. I'm being a total jerk," he said, stroking her cheek lightly. "I should be happy for you, and I am." He reached around the back of her neck and pulled her face toward him for a long, lingering kiss.

Elizabeth felt her tension dissipate immediately.

Then Todd pulled back and narrowed his eyes. "Are you sure all that fresh mountain air isn't going to make you hungry for male companionship?"

Elizabeth didn't answer his question in words. Instead she locked her lips against his for an even longer, more passionate kiss. *How can he even ask such a question?* Elizabeth wondered as she wrapped her arms tightly around Todd's strong

16

back. *I'm so in love with Todd, I can't even imagine being unfaithful. Doesn't he feel that?* "Just to prove how much I know I'll be thinking about you, I promise to write at least every other day," she whispered in his ear.

"I'll be looking forward to your letters," Todd said, nuzzling her neck.

"I just hope all those basketball jocks don't tease you when they see my letters in your mailbox all the time," Elizabeth said lovingly.

"Tease me? They wouldn't dare," Todd said. "And even if they do, I'll know it's just because they're jealous." He kissed her again.

Elizabeth kissed him back, savoring the feeling of his warm, soft lips on her own.

Chapter 2

"How much longer until we get there?" Jessica called up the front of the van, trying not to sound as impatient as she felt.

"The camp is right up ahead," Darlene, the driver, called back. "Just a few more minutes."

Jessica slumped back against her seat. She felt as if they had been driving on this incredibly windy road for hours. She looked at her watch and groaned. It was only forty-five minutes since the Camp Echo Mountain van had left the Billings, Montana, airport.

Elizabeth was sitting in the van's passenger seat, having an animated discussion with Darlene about the ecosystems of Montana's mountain forests. "Why do I see so many burned-out tree trunks?" Elizabeth asked.

"Last summer we had a pretty severe forest fire," Darlene replied.

"How awful!" Elizabeth cried.

"It's really not that awful. It's part of the cycle of the forest," Darlene explained. "The fire actually helps to rejuvenate the forest, cleaning the old, rotted plant life away to make room for new, fresh growth."

"How fascinating," Elizabeth said.

How fascinating, Jessica mimicked silently. *Sometimes Liz can get so excited about such boring things.* Not that anyone else was offering a more interesting conversation to divert Jessica's attention from her queasy stomach.

Lila was dozing, after nearly driving Jessica crazy by jabbering on and on about an article she had read describing the merits of mountain air on one's complexion.

The other JCs in the van were Justin Siena, a reasonably cute—if boring—guy from Fresno, California, and two guys from Sweet Valley High, Winston Egbert and Aaron Dallas. The three boys were involved in a conversation comparing northern California sports teams to southern California sports teams. At least, Justin and Aaron were involved in the conversation—Winston just kept cracking jokes.

"Did you hear the one about the quarterback and the umpire?" Winston prompted.

"The quarterback and the referee, Winston," Aaron corrected him. "Umpires are in baseball."

20

"Right, well, anyway," Winston continued. "A quarterback and an ump—a referee—are at a bar having a drink after the game when they spot two gorgeous girls sitting by themselves at a table. The quarterback puffs out his chest and stands up. 'I'll handle this,' he says, and he ambles over to their table.

"One minute later the referee sees one of the ladies throw her drink in the quarterback's face," Winston continued. "When the quarterback comes back to the bar and slinks down on his stool, the umpire jumps up and yells: 'Incomplete pass!'" Winston broke out into a fit of giggles.

Justin and Aaron groaned.

Jessica tuned out.

Finally the van emerged from the forest, and Jessica squinted against the suddenly bright sky. *Now that's more like it,* she thought as she looked down on the expansive valley spread out below them. *I'd been wondering why they call this the Big Sky State.*

The road gently curved its way down the bowl of the valley. Jessica looked out on a huge field of lush green grass speckled with yellow spots of blossoms. Across the field was a placid blue lake in the shape of a lima bean. A huge dark mountain loomed straight up behind the lake.

"Echo Mountain's straight up ahead!" Darlene sang out merrily.

Jessica let out an involuntary sigh. "It's beautiful," she whispered.

21

"It's huge!" Winston said.

Lila rubbed her eyes and yawned. "This is *it*?" she gasped. "But it's in the middle of nowhere!"

"Exactly," Darlene said enthusiastically.

Jessica could see a cluster of small wooden cabins arranged at either end of the lake. Directly in between them, opposite the mountain, was a massive log cabin with three stone chimneys. A quaint whitewashed house stood in the shadow of the log cabin.

"Where's the camp?" Lila demanded. "Where are the shops? Isn't there even a movie theater?"

"No shops, no movie theaters, no malls—not even a gas station within a ten-mile radius," Darlene continued. "Isn't it wonderful?"

"Fabulous!" Elizabeth chimed.

"Torture!" Lila whined.

The van drove by a wooden sign with the words CAMP ECHO MOUNTAIN painted in black. A few minutes later the van pulled up behind the huge log cabin.

"This is the main hall," Darlene said. "Lacey lives in that little white house, upstairs from the camp's office." Lacey Cavannah was the camp's owner.

"Do you believe this, Jess?" Lila cried as they climbed out of the van. "Did you have any idea we'd be stuck up here in the mountains like prisoners?"

Jessica laughed. "I think it would be more

healthy, Lila, to think of it as an oasis, not a prison."

Lila puffed out her lower lip and flipped her hair over her shoulder. "Sure, go ahead and laugh now, Jessica Wakefield. Let's see what you say after you've had two days without a real manicure," she said, crossing her arms tightly over her chest.

Jessica rolled her eyes. For some reason Lila sounded especially shallow to Jessica's ears today. *So it's not the most plush place in the world,* Jessica conceded. *But now that we're here, I wish Lila would stop complaining and make the most of it.*

"You two go ahead without me," Elizabeth said. "I want to take a minute to get myself settled here before my brain melts to mush in the sun."

"Suit yourself, Liz," Jessica said, reaching her arms around her back to hook together her bright green bikini top. "But it's the last chance we'll get to work on our tans in peace for a month."

"Do you have to remind me?" Lila grumbled as she fastened the waist strap of the floral-print sarong skirt that matched the print of her bikini.

"C'mon, Li—turn that frown upside down," Jessica said cheerily, giving Lila a jab on the cheek.

"Do you *want* me to smack you?" Lila asked sarcastically.

Jessica just laughed, throwing her towel over her shoulder as she headed off toward the lake.

23

"Why me?" Lila asked the sky. Then she trudged after Jessica's jaunty figure.

Elizabeth smiled and turned to the dark stillness of the cabin, surveying the sparse room. There were six beds, four lined up against the wall opposite the door and two against the other wall. Cheap plywood dressers and nightstands were crowded in between the beds, and faded red-and-white-flowered curtains hung limply on the windows.

Rustic was a generous description. *Run-down* was more like it.

Oh, well, we won't be spending much time in here anyway, Elizabeth reminded herself.

Unfortunately there was only one desk, jammed right next to the door. *Well, I'll just have to be selfish and claim it,* she decided quickly. *After all, if I'm going to write the camp play, I need my work space.*

Elizabeth didn't think anyone would mind if she rearranged some furniture, so she pushed one of the beds closer to the side wall and dragged the desk over to a window. She arranged her laptop computer, dictionary, thesaurus, and the book of poetry she brought for inspiration next to her computer. Something was missing. *Todd.* Elizabeth took his framed picture out of her bag and placed it next to the pile of books. Then she picked it up and gave it a quick kiss. She missed him already.

Pleased with her cozy writing area, Elizabeth

decided to change into her bathing suit and head to the lake to find her sister and Lila. After all, Maria wasn't going to be arriving until evening. Elizabeth had a whole afternoon to kill.

Elizabeth headed toward the center of camp. As she walked by a number of small cabins that were scattered around the main lodge, she remembered that Darlene had said most of the indoor workshops were held in these.

Elizabeth stopped walking when she heard yelling and shouting coming from inside one of the cabins.

"I've had it up to here with your lying, deceiving ways!" an angry baritone voice boomed out of the cabin's open door. "Give me one good reason why I shouldn't rip your throat right out of your neck!" Then the voice grew ominously dark. "Once I get my hands on you, you worthless piece of slime, I'm gonna make you wish you never crossed me."

Without thinking, Elizabeth raced into the cabin, ready to break up a fight.

"What's going on in here?" she screamed. Then she stopped short.

Standing alone in the middle of the room was the most gorgeous guy she'd ever seen. He was tall and muscular, with beautiful red lips and dark green eyes under thick black eyebrows. A three-day growth of stubble darkened his face, contrasting with his light brown hair that flopped over his forehead, almost hanging in his eyes.

The guy had stopped yelling and now stood panting for air.

"I'm sorry . . . if I scared you," he apologized, wiping his hand across his damp forehead. "I was just doing . . . some rage exercises."

"*Rage* exercises?" Elizabeth asked quizzically.

"I guess that sounds pretty weird," he said, laughing. "First things first—my name's Joey. Joey Mason." He held out his hand for Elizabeth to shake.

"Elizabeth Wakefield," Elizabeth said tentatively, grasping his hand. Even though it was damp with sweat, she couldn't help but notice how strong his long, graceful fingers were.

"I'm the drama counselor here," Joey continued. "I was just planning out my classes over the next few weeks. You caught me practicing 'Anger and Rage: Act It, Don't Overact It.'"

Elizabeth blushed. "I can't believe I made such a fuss when you were just acting," she said, feeling totally embarrassed.

"I'll take it as a compliment that my acting was convincing," Joey said with a grin. Then he gave her a warm smile. "Besides, I think it's sweet that you were so concerned," he added, his green eyes looking deep into hers.

Elizabeth felt her heart melt.

Joey looked at his watch. "Drat! I've got to go to

a meeting at Lacey's," he said. "I hope I'll get to see more of you, Elizabeth Wakefield." He smiled a friendly smile, then winked.

Elizabeth's heart was pounding so mightily, she couldn't even trust herself to speak. Watching Joey saunter off toward Lacey's white house, Elizabeth suddenly had the desire to sign up for acting workshops. Too bad she was at camp to help teach workshops, not take them.

Jessica and Lila had discovered that halfway between the girls' cabins and the center of camp there was a small strip of empty sand—perfect for an afternoon of sunbathing in peace. Even if it wasn't like the soft, sandy beaches of southern California, at least it was a beach, and a deserted one.

At first the sun's intense heat had felt wonderful. But it soon turned suffocating. *It feels like I'm wrapped inside an electric blanket turned on its highest setting,* Jessica thought. She couldn't figure it out. Usually she and Lila could withstand hours of sunbathing on the beach or by the pool. Yet after fifteen minutes Jessica almost felt ready to call it quits. *Is it just me,* she wondered, *or is this mountain sun too much of a good thing?*

Jessica raised herself on two elbows and looked over at Lila. "Li?"

Lila didn't open her eyes. "Hmmm?"

"Do you want to go in the shade?"

Now Lila opened her eyes, squinting against the white sun. "What, are you wimping out on me?" she asked.

"No. Of course not," Jessica said, lying back down. "I was just thinking about you. It seemed like you were really hot."

"Mmmhmmm," Lila mumbled. "It does feel hotter than back home, doesn't it?"

"Thank you!" Jessica said with a sigh. "I thought it was just me."

Then Jessica heard a familiar voice. "The sun *is* hotter up here, and more dangerous," Elizabeth said authoritatively. She was approaching the girls from the center of camp. "You'd better wear a lot of sunblock."

Lila propped herself up on her elbows. "You're telling me that just because we're a few thousand feet closer to the sun, it's stronger?" She flopped back down. "Nice try, Einstein," Lila snorted. "The sun's ninety-three *million* miles away—do you really think that a measly few thousand feet is going to make a difference? *Please.*"

Elizabeth rolled her eyes. "No, Lila," she said impatiently. "It's not the distance—it's the air quality. At this high elevation the air is thinner, so we're getting more of the sun's dangerous ultraviolet rays."

Lila turned her head to look up at Elizabeth. "Oh. Well, I guess that makes sense," she murmured.

28

"Anyway, what took *you* so long?" Jessica asked her sister.

Elizabeth smiled mysteriously, then stopped. "I stopped by the camp office to find out my JC duties," she said quickly.

"Oh, I totally forgot to do that," Jessica said. "Did you happen to notice what I got?"

"And me?" Lila asked.

Elizabeth smiled again. "I had a feeling you guys came straight here, so I checked your assignments, too."

"And—?" Jessica prompted her.

Elizabeth sat down on her towel. "All the JCs have been assigned responsibility for a group of six campers," she explained. "We'll be with these kids a lot—for all group activities, meals, and whatever." Elizabeth looked at the piece of paper in her hand. "Jess, you got a group of seven- and eight-year-olds. Lila, you got a group of thirteen-year-olds."

"Great," Lila said with a sigh. "The awkward age."

"Not all thirteen-year-olds are as awkward and gangly as you were at that age," Jessica teased, giving Lila a playful shove.

"Very funny, Wakefield. As I recall, you were no beauty queen yourself." Lila smirked.

"Oh, that's real supportive, you two," Elizabeth said in a scolding tone. "We're supposed to be mature role models for these youngsters."

Lila and Jessica looked at each other and rolled

their eyes. "So, Miss Role Model, what'd you get?" Jessica asked.

"I got ten-year-olds," Elizabeth answered. Then she continued with her description of their work assignments. "We're also supposed to assist with one particular workshop for the whole month. So we'll all have contact with all the campers as they rotate through the different activities."

Jessica rolled onto her stomach. "Oh, joy," she grumbled as the reality of the coming month became more clear. *Why in the world did I agree to do this?* she asked herself. *I don't even like kids.* And in Jessica's experience, the feeling seemed to be mutual. Like when Lila tricked her into being a Kiddie Kounselor at Lila's uncle's Caribbean resort, Club Paradise, Jessica had been assigned the worst kids in the whole place, and she had suffered tremendously. And that had only been one week. This was a whole *month*.

"Why such a glum face, Jess?" Lila asked, smirking.

Jessica sat up and plastered on a smile—she didn't want to encourage Lila's negative attitude. "Who's glum? I can't wait to spend time with a bunch of impressionable kids," she said airily. "It'll be my opportunity to teach about the finer things in life. Like boys and shopping."

"Actually, Jess, you've been assigned to teach the dance workshop," Elizabeth informed her.

"Really?" Jessica asked. "That's the best news I've gotten all day!" She suddenly felt positive again.

"What'd I get?" Lila asked.

Elizabeth looked down at the paper in her hands. "You got arts and crafts," she answered.

Lila stretched out her legs. "Phew. For once someone actually paid attention to what I filled in as my preference."

Elizabeth tossed a pebble into the lake. "I got sailing."

"Sailing?" Jessica cried. "You get to learn how to sail, Liz. That sounds fun."

"Actually I was kind of disappointed that I didn't get acting. It looks like that will be a good workshop." Elizabeth tossed another pebble into the lake.

Jessica looked at her sister. *Since when is Liz interested in acting?* she wondered. Then she thought she detected a blush crossing her sister's face. Jessica smelled something fishy. "You've never thought about acting before, Liz. Why the change of heart?"

Elizabeth opened and closed her mouth. "Um, well, I—" she sputtered.

"Yes?" Jessica asked.

"I just thought it might be fun to try something new," Elizabeth said unconvincingly.

Jessica took a stab. "Might this have anything to do with a gorgeous acting counselor?"

Elizabeth's eyes opened wide and the words tumbled out. "Oh, my gosh! Did you see him, too? Isn't he the most beautiful man you've ever seen?"

Jessica laughed, tapping a finger on her forehead. "No, just using my impressive powers of deductive reasoning."

Lila laughed and Elizabeth's blush deepened.

"So are you interested in this guy?" Jessica prodded.

"Don't be ridiculous, Jess. I'm not even in the market," Elizabeth said quickly, wiping a bead of sweat from her brow. "I saw him practicing some exercises and he seemed to really know what he was doing."

"Mmmhmmm," Lila said, giggling.

Elizabeth flipped her ponytail. "Aside from the fact that I have a boyfriend, I'd never be interested in Joey," Elizabeth claimed. "He's one of those weird actor types."

But as Elizabeth fussed with her towel, Jessica noticed she was still blushing furiously. Jessica watched her sister lie down and close her eyes. The world's most faithful girlfriend, Elizabeth usually wasn't so easily flustered by another guy. *Either there's something wrong in the happy-loving-couple-land of Liz and Todd or this guy Joey is extremely hot,* Jessica mused. *Or maybe both.*

Jessica lay back down and closed her eyes to the heat of the sun. *This new development could be just the thing to make this month quite interesting,* she realized. After all, since Jessica had decided to have a boyless summer, at least Elizabeth's potentially hot situation would provide a little of the drama and intrigue Jessica loved.

Lila and Jess are either into self-torture or they've transformed into cold-blooded reptiles, Elizabeth said to herself as she walked back toward camp. After nearly melting in the heat, Elizabeth had left Lila and Jessica to bake. She wanted to see Maria as soon as she arrived.

Now as Elizabeth walked through the center of camp she saw that work had begun. *Should I offer to help?* Elizabeth wondered as she watched people rush from building to building, carrying bins of food, pots and pans, signs and easels, and other assorted supplies. Lacey stood on the porch of her house, barking out directives and orders.

"Peter! Bring the firewood to the back of the shed! Suzanne! Set up the menus in the kitchen! Bernard! Watch what you're doing! You drop that barrel and we'll all bathe in bug juice!"

Elizabeth smiled. *I'd probably get in the way,* she decided. She continued toward the girls' camp.

When she got back to the cabin, Elizabeth heard a rustle of activity inside. *Maybe that's Maria!* Elizabeth thought. But her hopeful anticipation was cut short as soon as her eyes adjusted to the dark cabin. A tough-looking girl with a dark red baseball cap worn backward on her head was throwing Elizabeth's books and supplies into a cardboard box.

Elizabeth felt her skin crawl. "What do you think you're doing?" she demanded. "Those are my things!"

At the sound of Elizabeth's voice the girl looked up from where she was crouched, down next to the wall outlet. Without taking her eyes off Elizabeth in the doorway, she unplugged the cord to Elizabeth's computer and started coiling it around in a circle. She looked Elizabeth up and down slowly, then lowered her eyelids. "Sorry about your things," the girl said with complete insincerity. "But since I'm writing the silly camp play, I need this whole desk for myself." She tossed the computer cord into the box.

The girl's voice was deep and gruff, and she spoke with an accent that Elizabeth couldn't quite place. "That's funny," Elizabeth said, trying to sound casual to cover her irritation. "I was planning on writing the play."

The girl gave Elizabeth a dismissive smile and shrugged. "I'm surprised they didn't tell you about the little contest," she said as she picked up Elizabeth's picture of Todd and glanced at it. She chuckled and threw it into the box.

Elizabeth bristled. "Contest? What contest?"

"Whoever writes the best play first gets it produced," the girl explained, stripping down to a bright orange string bikini. "So don't even bother. *I'm* the best writer here. In fact, Joey told me he'd just as soon slit his wrists as have to produce a play written by some *amateur* at this camp." The girl pushed past Elizabeth and sauntered out of the cabin.

Elizabeth's heart skipped a beat at the sound of Joey's name. *Is she his girlfriend?* she wondered with a pang of jealousy.

Watching the girl's hips sway down the road to the lake, Elizabeth was overcome with hostility. For the first time in her life, Elizabeth was experiencing hate at first sight.

Chapter 3

Elizabeth stood sweating over a huge basin of steaming hot water. After the horrible scene back in the cabin, she had decided to do something useful. The kitchen staff was preparing for a huge barbecue to welcome all the JCs that night, and they needed someone to clean off the trays that had been sitting in storage all winter.

The sound of steel trays banging against the steel sink clamored inside Elizabeth's brain. But clamoring even louder was that obnoxious girl's annoying voice. *I'm the best writer here,* her voice grated.

Elizabeth sprayed the trays stacked up in the deep sink with a powerful stream of water and watched the suds disappear down the drain. She couldn't remember ever feeling so much immediate hatred toward someone she barely knew.

Elizabeth had always been proud of her open-minded approach to new people, and she usually gave even the most seemingly disagreeable people the benefit of the doubt. Sometimes it took more effort than at other times, but usually she succeeded in finding something redeeming in everyone. Elizabeth looked at the growing stack of clean trays. *Maybe this girl is just insecure and hides behind a screen of bravado*, Elizabeth thought. *Maybe I should give her a second chance.*

Then Elizabeth heard the grating voice in her head again. *Joey told me he'd just as soon slit his wrists as have to produce a play written by some* amateur *at this camp.*

She is definitely the most obnoxious person I have ever met in my life, Elizabeth fumed. *I'm no saint, but I bet even Mother Theresa wouldn't be able to find anything redeeming in that girl.*

"Liz? Is that you?" Elizabeth jumped when she heard a voice that was both familiar and unfamiliar. She turned to see Maria standing in the doorway of the kitchen.

"Maria!" Elizabeth pulled her arms out of the soapy water, tugging the rubber gloves she was wearing off her hands. In doing so she managed to spray both herself and Maria with drops of soap and hot water.

"Watch it!" Maria said. But she was laughing as she brushed the soap off the front of her white linen shirt and khaki-colored jodhpurs.

"I'm sorry," Elizabeth said, laughing, too. "Now that we're both wet, come here and give me a hug!" The girls hugged for a long time, rocking from side to side.

Then Elizabeth took a step back to get a look at her old friend. The strikingly pretty African American girl had grown a number of inches, so Elizabeth had to lift her face to meet Maria's eyes. Maria's curly black hair was cropped short, giving her a more sophisticated look. But otherwise she looked quite the same—an older, more gorgeous version of her younger self. "I can't tell you how wonderful it is to see you," Elizabeth said. "You look totally the same as you did, but somehow different. I mean—"

Maria laughed. "I know exactly what you mean," she said, leaning back against the steel sink. "It feels like a time warp, you know? A lot has happened in the past three years, but seeing you, it's like we're thirteen again, like we were never separated."

Elizabeth nodded eagerly. "It is, isn't it," she agreed. "We're going to have a great summer, aren't we?"

Maria took Elizabeth's hand and gave it a squeeze. "We sure are."

Just then Bernard, the head cook, walked into the dishwashing area. "How are those trays coming?" Then he noticed Maria. "Sorry. I didn't know you were receiving visitors," he said, his merry eyes twinkling over his bushy brown beard.

"It's okay, Bernard," Elizabeth said warmly. "This is my good friend Maria—Maria Slater. We haven't seen each other since middle school."

Bernard held out his hand and Maria shook it. "Good to meet you, Maria. I'm in charge of the food around here. So don't even think about complaining," he said, puffing out his chest to look menacing.

Elizabeth giggled. Bernard was one of the sweetest, most unintimidating men she had ever met. On the van ride to camp Darlene had given Elizabeth the rundown on Bernard. He had been head cook at Camp Echo Mountain for the last eight years. He loved being around kids and the kids loved him, so Lacey kept him on, even though he wasn't the most skilled chef. "Oh, Bernard. We wouldn't dream of complaining," Elizabeth said.

Maria wagged a finger at him in mock warning. "As long as you don't give us reason to complain."

Bernard smiled. "You two are going to love the food. Tonight we have a wonderful chicken barbecue—with all the fixin's."

"Yum," Maria said, patting her belly. "Sounds terrific."

"I was just finishing rinsing off the rest of these

trays here before Maria so rudely interrupted me," Elizabeth joked.

Maria laughed. "Why don't you go ahead and finish up," she said. "I want to see if I can find where that girl Nicole has disappeared to so I can introduce you. I've been dying for you two to meet."

"Go ahead. I'll be here, slaving over the hot sink!" Elizabeth said.

"I'll be back!" Maria called cheerfully as she trotted out of the kitchen. The screen door squeaked and slammed shut behind her.

"Let me know when you're done," Bernard said after Maria had left.

"Mmmhmmm, sure," Elizabeth said, turning back to the sink. She pulled on the rubber gloves and smiled. She had been playing a little game with herself, trying to figure out whether any of the girls she had seen today was Maria's friend. She ran through the possibilities. *Maybe it's that bubbly redhead I saw reading a book by the boathouse. Or that pretty Asian girl I saw going for a run in the woods.*

She rinsed the last tray and remembered to shake the water from her gloves this time before taking them off. She was just about to set off to find Bernard to tell him she was done when she heard Maria's voice drift through the kitchen's open door. Then she heard another voice that sounded familiar. *That must be Nicole,* she thought, smiling in anticipation of meeting Maria's friend.

Elizabeth's smile faded abruptly when she saw who was with Maria. It was the obnoxious girl from the cabin.

"Elizabeth, meet my good friend Nicole Banes," Maria said, smiling broadly. "Nicole, this is the Elizabeth Wakefield I've told you so much about." She held open the screen door as Nicole waltzed inside the kitchen.

Nicole looked Elizabeth up and down, her lips curled up into a faint sneer. "Hi."

Elizabeth bristled. "Hi."

Nicole held out her hand as if she expected Elizabeth to kiss it.

Reluctantly Elizabeth took Nicole's hand and shook it stiffly. At the girl's cold touch Elizabeth felt her jubilant mood disappear.

I can't believe this is happening, she thought.

Jessica was famished, but the plate of food in front of her left much to be desired. Her potato salad looked like it had been made with more mayonnaise than potatoes—it was runny and inedible. Her corn had been scorched black on the barbecue. And her chicken breast was so poorly cooked that its surface splintered like wood when she touched it, while the inside was still bright pink.

42

Looks like I'll be losing weight this month, Jessica thought as she took a sip of her bug juice. She grimaced at the syrupy-sweet taste. "Ughhh," she said out loud. "This stuff is foul."

"I know. I refuse to let that filth cross my lips," Lila said, her mouth curled in disdain. "Not only is it crammed with sugar and calories, I think it could do serious damage to your stomach lining. I'm thinking about having my father send me a couple cases of Evian."

Jessica smiled. Only Lila would think of having water bottled in the French Alps airlifted to the mountains of Montana.

Lila stabbed at her potato salad with a plastic fork. "I swear, I haven't felt this juvenile since the third grade when Ms. Woods used to split the classroom down the middle. Boys on one side, girls on the other," she griped. All the female junior and senior counselors were having a "get to know you" barbecue on the girls' side of camp while the boys were having a barbecue on their side of camp. Suzanne, the camp's art counselor, had explained Lacey's reasoning for the separate barbecues to Jessica and Lila when they had met her earlier that afternoon. Supposedly Lacey felt that if the groups were mixed, everyone would be so fixated on flirting with the opposite sex that they wouldn't relax and make friends with each other. Jessica had to admit that Lacey was probably right.

Now Jessica watched somewhat longingly as the other female counselors mixed and mingled around the barbecue. Lila had plopped herself down at an out-of-the way table, saying that she wasn't in the mood to mix with the other girls. Jessica had reluctantly joined her. *This is the last time I'll indulge Lila's moodiness,* Jessica decided. *Otherwise she'll be an impossible spoiled brat all month.* "It's not that bad, Li," Jessica said out loud. "It looks like there might be some really nice girls here. Maybe we should get to know them."

Lila looked across the table at Jessica and rolled her eyes. "I didn't come here to make friends, Jess. Maybe a boyfriend or two . . . but that's not going to happen tonight." She sat sulking silently.

Jessica took another stab at changing her friend's mood. "Look on the bright side, Li. At least Winston Egbert isn't here to give the whole of southern California a bad name," Jessica said with a laugh.

"Ohmigosh!" Lila exclaimed, slapping her forehead with the back of her hand. "I thought I was going to die of embarrassment this afternoon when Winston tripped and fell right on top of that girl at the lake. Isn't that her over there?" Lila gestured to a table a few yards away.

Jessica followed Lila's gaze. She spotted the girl who had been wearing a bright orange bikini earlier. Jessica had thought that she and Lila were bold in their bikinis, but this girl looked like she had walked straight off the cover of the *Sports Illustrated* swimsuit edition.

Now the girl looked a lot sportier, wearing a navy polo T-shirt and a red baseball cap worn backward. "She looks a lot different now that she's got some clothes on," Jessica said.

"That girl next to her sure is gorgeous," Lila said. "Doesn't she look like a model?"

Jessica looked at the pretty black girl. There was something about her that looked amazingly familiar. Then Jessica realized with a start that she was looking at a grown-up Maria Slater. "That's Maria!" Jessica exclaimed. "And that must be the friend she was telling Elizabeth about."

"Well, she doesn't look *that much* like a model," Lila said dismissively.

Jessica smiled. She knew Lila had never cared much for Maria. It was probably because Maria had always been extremely successful at teasing Lila. Lila wasn't the type of person who could laugh at herself, and she really hated to be the butt of someone else's joke.

If anyone will be able to keep Lila in line this summer, it's Maria, Jessica thought. *But where's Liz? Why isn't she sitting with her two new best friends?*

As if on cue, Elizabeth suddenly appeared at their table. "Can I join you guys?" she asked.

"Sure," Jessica said.

Elizabeth sat down.

"Why don't you have a plate? Aren't you eating?" Jessica asked.

Elizabeth fiddled with a small twig. "I'm not hungry."

Jessica looked at her sister's gloomy expression, realizing immediately that something was seriously bothering her sister. Elizabeth usually devoured barbecue food, even when it was disgusting like tonight's fare. *What's going on?* Jessica wondered.

Then she saw Elizabeth glower in the direction of Maria Slater and the bikini girl. *Hmmm,* Jessica thought. *Time for a little investigative questioning.* "That's Maria Slater over there, isn't it? Have you gotten a chance to talk to her yet?" Jessica asked.

Elizabeth nodded. "Yeah, this afternoon," she said quickly.

"Is that the friend she was telling you about?" Jessica asked.

"Yeah," Elizabeth responded.

Clearly Elizabeth wasn't going to volunteer any more details. Jessica would have to be relentless. "Why aren't you sitting with them? I thought Maria really wanted you to meet her."

"I met her already. Her name's Nicole," Elizabeth said, her voice dripping with disgust.

Jessica raised an eyebrow but said nothing. Her twin's tone of voice told her all she needed to know.

Lila, an avid fan of strife and conflict—especially when it involved other people—clearly wanted to know more. "Should we take that to mean you and this Nicole girl didn't quite hit it off?" she asked.

Elizabeth looked at Lila's gossip-hungry face. "We just—" she started, then stopped. *What can I say?* Elizabeth asked herself. *That I hated Nicole on sight?* First of all, Elizabeth wasn't very proud of the way the meeting had gone, especially since Maria had expected them to hit it off. Besides, Elizabeth knew that if Lila heard the full story, it would get back to Maria in no time.

Just then Lacey Cavannah marched to the center of the tables and banged a metal spoon against a pot, bringing the buzz of the girls' conversations to an abrupt stop.

Elizabeth sighed with relief, happy for the excuse not to answer Lila's intrusive question. "I guess we'd better pay attention," she said, enjoying the look of disappointment on Lila's expectant face.

"Listen up, girls!" Lacey bellowed. "I'd like to take this opportunity to officially welcome you all to Camp Echo Mountain," she pronounced in her high-pitched southern drawl. "I hope you've had a pleasant afternoon and an enjoyable dinner because it's the last moment of freedom you'll have for the rest of the month. The campers start arriving tomorrow at oh-seven-hundred hours."

47

"What is this, boot camp?" Jessica whispered to her sister.

Elizabeth smiled. Jessica's joke was right on the money. Lacey even looked like a military leader, dressed all in khaki from the wide-brimmed fedora on her head, to her brass-buckled belt, to the beige-colored sensible shoes on her feet.

"Now's the time to lay down some rules," Lacey continued. "No mixed company in the cabins, no late-night carousing, no sneaking across the lake or into town, and I know I don't even have to tell you that there will be absolutely *no* alcohol or drugs at my camp," Lacey preached. "I'll have you girls know, I've just come from giving this speech to the boys, so don't accuse me of being sexist," she said, her lips pursed.

"And if any of you disobey the rules, there will be a grave price to pay," she warned. Lacey went on to describe the JCs' responsibilities in exhaustive detail, repeating the information that Elizabeth had gathered that afternoon. Besides helping out with workshops and watching over their assigned campers, the JCs had to attend the morning and evening flag ceremonies and perform at least one food-serving or cleanup duty a day. The assignments for those duties would be posted every morning outside the camp office.

Elizabeth paid closer attention when she heard a switch in Lacey's tone of voice. "But there will be fun to be had as well," Lacey was saying. "At the end of the month all the campers and counselors will take part in a day-long color war—a camp Olympics. So start brushing up on your physical prowess now," she announced happily.

Elizabeth leaned into Jessica. "I hope I get picked to be a team leader," she whispered. "It seems like so much fun."

Lila gave Elizabeth a patronizing look. "Thrills-ville," she said sarcastically.

Jessica nudged Lila's elbow. "Lighten up, Li," she whispered.

Good for you, Jess, Elizabeth said silently, glad to see that Lila's negative attitude was getting to her twin, too.

Then Bernard appeared from the darkness, carrying bags and boxes.

"Oh, there you are, Bernard," Lacey said when she saw him. She turned back to the girls around the campfire. "Seeing as this is your last night of freedom, we've arranged to have a dessert feast: s'mores!" Lacey said triumphantly, looking as if she had granted the JCs a night of pure ecstasy. "So I will leave you kids to your roasting. Bernard, commence with the distribution of the marshmallows," she instructed. Then she turned and marched away from the picnic area.

"Whoop-de-doo," Lila sulked. "S'mores."

"I love s'mores!" Elizabeth exclaimed. "Don't you, Jess?"

"Um, sure," Jessica muttered.

Elizabeth scanned the crowd. Most of the girls seemed to share Lila and Jessica's lack of enthusiasm. Determined not to sink back into her earlier depression, Elizabeth realized she needed to do something to improve the spirits of the group.

An idea popped quickly into her head. "How about everyone joining together to sing our favorite songs from the camps we all went to as kids?" Elizabeth suggested cheerfully.

Nicole snorted scornfully in Elizabeth's direction. "How quaint," she said. "But really, do we want to sit around like a bunch of children eating s'mores and singing silly songs?"

Elizabeth felt her face flush as a chorus of titters broke out at a nearby table. "Do you have anything better to suggest?" she asked hotly.

Nicole flashed an evil smile. "I think a game of Truth or Dare would be a little more exciting." A number of girls nodded their agreement.

Elizabeth looked Nicole straight in the eye. "Sure. I'll go first," she said without even stopping to think.

"Liz!" Jessica whispered, nudging Elizabeth's knee.

Elizabeth ignored her, keeping her sights fixed on Nicole.

"Truth or dare?" Nicole asked tauntingly.

Elizabeth shuddered to imagine the "truth" question she might get. "A dare," she heard herself say. Nobody spoke as Nicole and Elizabeth locked their eyes in a standoff. Elizabeth's heart pounded. *I'll do whatever she says, without hesitation,* Elizabeth told herself resolutely. *I'll show her I can be just as tough as she thinks she is.*

Without taking her eyes off Nicole, Elizabeth couldn't help but notice Maria's distraught expression as she looked from Nicole to Elizabeth, biting her lip. Elizabeth felt a wave of regret. *So much for the Three Musketeers,* she thought, remembering Jessica's words.

Suddenly the silence was interrupted by the sound of footsteps and crackling twigs from the dark woods that surrounded the campfire. Squinting against the darkness, Elizabeth made out a number of ghostly white figures flitting through the trees. Her heart raced. *What's out there?* she wondered. More ghostly figures appeared and Elizabeth heard herself shriek. Other shrieks quickly joined hers.

All of a sudden Elizabeth heard laughter, then guffaws. "It's the guys!" someone shouted.

"Shhh! Don't let Lacey hear you!" someone else hissed.

Within seconds Elizabeth saw about twenty guys emerge from under white sheets. Most of them headed straight for the food table.

"Cool! More food!" Elizabeth heard Aaron Dallas say. "They never give us enough."

Then Joey stepped into the light of the campfire. "Boys! Everyone! There'll be time for feasting later. First we have to tell the girls about the grand traditions of Camp Echo Mountain."

"What kind of traditions?" Maria asked.

"The tradition of getting around Lacey's annoying rules!" Joey answered.

Everyone cheered.

Joey continued. "Kitchen raids, sneaking into town after dark, midnight canoe trips." Joey shook his hair out of his eyes and stared straight at Elizabeth.

Elizabeth gasped and looked away. Her heart swelled and her throat felt tight. She couldn't remember ever feeling so overcome with yearning. And confusion.

How can I feel this way about another guy when I'm so in love with Todd? she wondered.

Lila tuned out as Joey droned on and on about some pathetic acts of rebellion. She couldn't see what Elizabeth found so attractive about this guy. In Lila's opinion Joey tried much too hard to be cool. *But then, Elizabeth has never had much taste when it comes to men,* Lila thought, thinking of boring-as-milk Todd Wilkins.

Lila looked around the flickering light of the campfire for something to distract her. Then she let out an involuntary gasp. Sitting across the fire, a guy had inadvertently pulled off his shirt as he was taking off his ghost costume. *What a bod!* Lila thought, admiring his impressive ripple of chest and stomach muscles.

As if he heard her silent compliment, the guy looked straight at Lila. Lila stopped breathing when she felt his eyes bore into hers. He winked. Right then and there, Lila decided he would be hers. *And I'll do whatever it takes to get him,* she vowed.

Suddenly Lila's view of the guy was blocked. It was Jessica. "Lila? Do you want to come with us to get some s'mores?"

Lila raised her eyebrows in disdain. "Give me a break," she said with a grimace. "I haven't eaten s'mores since I was a child."

Jessica shrugged. "Suit yourself," she said, joining Elizabeth at the campfire.

Lila sat motionless on her bench, trying to will the boy with the amazing abdominal muscles to come over and talk to her. Lila Fowler would only make the first move as a last resort—guys should always come to her.

"Hi! What's your name?" Startled, Lila looked up to see two gangly teenage boys. One of them wore thick glasses, the other had braces on his teeth. Both of them had smudges of chocolate around their mouths.

Lila grimaced in disgust. "Lila," she said stiffly.

53

"I'm Buford," said the one in glasses. He pointed to the one standing next to him. "This is Johansen."

"Hi," Johansen said, waving his forearm in a stiff arc.

Unbelievable. "Are those your real names?" Lila asked.

They both broke out in giggles. "Our real *last* names," they said in unison.

"We're both named Steve, so our mothers have been calling us by our last names since we were little kids," Buford explained.

"We grew up next door to each other in Pittsburgh," Johansen added.

"Charming," Lila said, looking pointedly away. She hoped they would get the hint.

They didn't.

"Where're you from, Lila?" Johansen asked, letting his tongue roll around her name in a way that made Lila feel nauseated.

"Listen, I've got a splitting headache," Lila said. "I'm not in the mood to talk."

"Oh, sorry," Buford said.

"Sorry," Johansen echoed. They shuffled away.

Thank goodness, Lila thought, turning her attention back to Mr. Fabulous Abs. But he seemed content to be munching on the s'more that one of the other guys had handed him. *Why won't he come talk to me? Can't he see that I want to talk to*

54

him? And that I'm gorgeous? Lila thought, frustrated. *Maybe he's not getting my signals clearly enough in the dim light of the fire,* she reasoned. *That must be it.*

A drumbeat suddenly sounded from across the lake. As quickly as the boys arrived they jumped up and gathered their sheets, disappearing through the woods toward the lake.

Lila jumped up from the picnic table and scrambled into the woods. *I won't sleep a wink tonight if I don't at least exchange names with Mr. Fabulous,* Lila realized. *I'll do whatever it takes.*

Lila heard Jessica calling after her. "Li! Where are you going?"

But Lila didn't stop to explain—she didn't have any time to waste. Lila felt her way through the trees, coming out of the darkness to see the glow of moonlight on the lake. She looked at the group of anonymous dark figures lowering themselves from the dock into the waiting canoes. She had to find her guy. But she couldn't see a thing in the silver light.

Then she saw his distinctive broad shoulders lowering his body into a waiting canoe. *I'll do whatever it takes.* Without thinking how desperate it might make her look, Lila raced down the dock, pushing past the guys who were still finding their way toward their canoes.

"Let's go," someone said from inside her guy's canoe.

"Wait!" Lila wailed. She couldn't help herself. She reached down to grab the guy's shoulder before he disappeared into the night.

Startled, he looked up to her on the dock.

"What's your name?" Lila whispered, crouching down toward him.

He reached an arm up and touched her cheek. "People call me Bo," he said. Then the boat pushed off and he disappeared into the dark.

Lila stood up numbly, holding her hand to her cheek. It felt warm to the touch. She shivered. *Now I know why I let Jessica persuade me to come to this silly camp,* Lila said to herself. *To find my destiny.*

Elizabeth stood alone in the bathroom, watching herself in the mirror as she brushed her teeth. *Do I look like the kind of girl who would cheat on her boyfriend?* she asked her reflection. *No,* she answered herself.

So then why do I feel like one? she wondered morosely.

Utterly confused, Elizabeth spit toothpaste out into the sink. She bent down to drink directly out of the faucet, something she didn't normally do. But Elizabeth didn't feel like her normal self anyway.

Then she heard a painfully familiar voice. "Oh, gross," Nicole said. "Do you mind not wrapping your lips around the faucet? We all have to use that sink."

Elizabeth groaned. Why did Nicole have to have such amazingly bad timing? She stood up to see Nicole traipse into the bathroom, wearing a crisply ironed blue-and-white-striped cotton robe. She looked pristine and clean. *Too clean*, Elizabeth thought. In fact, with her cropped pixieish haircut and natural, outdoorsy looks, Nicole resembled the very image of the innocent girl next door. *Looks can be deceiving*, Elizabeth reminded herself.

"I saw you making eyes at Joey tonight," Nicole said as she took a position at the sink next to Elizabeth. "You better not even *think* about going after him. You don't have a chance." She squirted a perfect dollop of blue toothpaste onto her fuchsia toothbrush.

Elizabeth wiped her mouth with her towel. "And why not?" she asked, worried that Nicole would say Joey was her boyfriend.

"Because I want him and I'm going to get him," Nicole answered matter-of-factly.

So she's not Joey's girlfriend, Elizabeth thought with a smile. "We'll just see about that," she said out loud. Then she heard what she'd just said. *I'm not even sure what I feel about Joey*, Elizabeth realized with a start. *Besides, I've got Todd at home. Why did I rise so quickly to her challenge?*

Nicole dropped some lotion onto her fingertips.

57

"You can hold on to your childish fantasy if you like," she said, spreading the lotion on her cheeks. "And by the way—I know you think that you and Maria will be friends, but you're wrong. She's my friend and an extremely loyal one, I might add."

This was more than Elizabeth could take. "I was friends with Maria way before you even met her!" she railed, her face flushed with anger and frustration.

Nicole's thin lips curled into a sneer. "Well, Ms. Elizabeth Wakefield," she said, zipping up her toiletry bag. "It looks like the two of us are going to have our own little war—one without rules."

Just then Maria walked into the bathroom.

Nicole's sneer vanished. "Hi, Maria," she said sweetly.

"Oh, there you are—I've been looking for you," Maria said. She looked from Nicole to Elizabeth. "I'm glad to see you two are getting to know each other. I just knew you'd get along."

Elizabeth tried to smile.

Chapter 4

Lila looked at herself in the mirror of the deserted girls' bathroom and almost screamed. She had sneaked out of the cabin early Sunday morning while the other girls were still sleeping to get some solitude for her morning ritual. After all, she had to look absolutely divine today for her first daylight meeting with Bo.

And now she was facing a disaster. Her eyes were puffy from the terrible night's sleep she'd suffered on the thin, lumpy mattress. The dry mountain air made her straight, silky hair look flat and stringy. And the broken window screens had done nothing to keep the bugs from attacking her face, which was dotted with red blotches.

It's a good thing I allowed extra time, she said to herself. *I have to transform myself back into the Lila Fowler I know and love.* But her usual combination of artistry would look too unnatural here in the mountains. No, she had to apply her makeup so deftly that it would look almost as if she wasn't wearing any at all.

Lila covered the circles under her eyes and the bug bites with a few dabs of concealer. Then she brushed on a liberal coating of loose powder and touched her eyelashes with a bit of brown mascara.

She took a step back to examine the results. Gorgeous, but just a little shy of devastating. *The eyes need more*, she realized. Lila rummaged through her bag and found that all she had was brown liquid eyeliner. A little risky, but it would have to do.

Now for the hair. Lila bent over at the waist and teased the underside of her hair, spraying it with a light mist of hair spray. She flipped her hair over her head and looked in the mirror, puckering her lips at her reflection.

She looked better than good. She looked fabulous.

But what would she wear?

Back in the girls' cabin most of the girls were stumbling around, pulling on T-shirts and shorts. Jessica was still buried under the covers.

Lila yanked Jessica's blanket. "Jess, you've got to help me plan a knockout outfit!"

Jessica grabbed the blanket and buried herself. "Leave me alone."

"But I need some help building the outfit that will make Bo fall in love with me!"

Maria and Nicole were just heading out of the cabin for the bathroom. "Why don't you just wear your checkbook?" Maria teased. "That's what you usually do to attract guys."

Nicole laughed. "Oooh, that's harsh."

Lila fumed. *Why can't I ever think of a snappy comeback to Maria?* she thought. *I must have Bo on the brain.*

"I can't believe you let Maria get away with that," Jessica said to Lila after Nicole and Maria had left.

Lila put her hands on her hips. "You clearly don't understand what I'm going through here," she said. "I've been given my one chance at happiness this summer, and I don't even know what to wear!"

Jessica rolled her eyes. "I can't believe you're getting so boy crazy already," she grumbled as she walked over to her dresser. "Just throw on a T-shirt and shorts." She looked at Lila's eyes closely. "And lighten up on the eyeliner next time."

Lila frowned. "There was a time when you didn't think being boy crazy was all that crazy," she said, looking with disapproval as Jessica pulled on a faded blue crew neck T-shirt and baggy khaki shorts. "Lighten up—have some fun. There are lots of cute guys here." *Not that they'll notice you in that outfit,* she added to herself.

Jessica finished tying her sneakers in silence. "I'm ready, so hurry up and decide what you want to wear or we'll miss breakfast."

"Jess, you might consider changing into something a little more—" Lila paused. "A little less—"

"What?" Jessica demanded. "What's wrong with what I'm wearing?"

"Well, it's not up to your usual high standards, Jess," Lila said gingerly. She knew that her best friend wasn't very good at taking criticism, especially when it concerned fashion.

"I think I look fine," Jessica said resolutely.

Lila raised her eyebrows. She hated to see her friend fall to pieces. *Jess is definitely not herself,* she realized. *And it's up to me to get her back to normal.* Lila vowed to help Jessica find a guy this summer. It was high time she got over Christian. And Ken.

But first Lila had to line up her guy. She picked out an outfit on her own: a periwinkle blue short-sleeve raw silk romper with pearl buttons. "C'mon, Jess," she said after she'd dressed. "Let's get to the mess hall." *And find Bo,* she added silently.

"Isn't that your dreamboat dumping his tray?" Jessica asked when they entered the mess hall.

Lila watched forlornly as Bo and two other guys scraped off their trays and left the mess hall. Lila heard an unwelcome voice behind her.

"Love your outfit, Lila," Maria said in a loud voice as she walked into the mess hall with Nicole. "But you'd better watch out for grass stains. They're murder to get out of raw silk—or is that linen?"

"It's silk," Lila replied archly.

Lacey, who was sitting at a nearby table, looked up at Lila. "You're wearing silk on your first day at camp? I suggest you get changed before the campers arrive."

Lila groaned. "I will, Lacey, right after breakfast," she told the camp owner. She noticed a couple of counselors snickering.

Thanks a lot, Maria, Lila thought.

"Those aren't children, those are monsters!" Jessica cried as she looked out the window. A vanload of young campers had just arrived, and the JCs stood watching the chaotic scene from the counselors' recreation room in the main lodge.

"They're just cranky after the long ride. I'm sure they'll be better once they've settled in," Elizabeth said, trying to convince herself as well as her sister.

As Lacey had explained the night before, arrival at sleep-away camp was always a traumatic event for children. Once the campers had overcome the initial trauma, Elizabeth and the other JCs would meet them in the mess hall for lunch.

"I'm just glad we don't have to deal with them yet," said Angela Davis, a pretty, dark-haired Latina from New York who had arrived with Maria and Nicole.

"I can tell you right now, if my kids know what's good for them, they're going to behave with decency and respect," Nicole declared.

"And what if they don't?" Elizabeth asked.

"They just will," Nicole said, staring at Elizabeth defiantly.

"Nicole's really good with kids," Maria said quickly, evidently trying to defuse some of the tension.

"I'm sure she is," Elizabeth said. *Good at terrorizing them*, she added silently.

The conflict between the girls was interrupted by a commotion outside.

"Where's my mommy!" a little girl in brown pigtails screamed as she jumped off the bus. She dropped the doll in her hand onto the ground and stood frozen in the doorway of the bus. "I want my mommy!" she bawled, tears streaming down her face.

A little blond boy with freckles jumped off the bus next. "Your mommy doesn't want you!" he said maliciously. "That's why she sent you here!" He barreled into the sobbing girl's unmoving figure and she crumpled to the ground, erupting into shrill spasms of shrieks.

Watching these children, Elizabeth felt a little

sorry for her sister. While Elizabeth was usually able to establish an easy, respectful rapport with children, Jessica seemed to repel them. And Jessica had been assigned these kids, the youngest campers in the whole camp. Elizabeth felt a little guilty about it, but she was relieved that her charges, who were arriving later that morning, were a little older.

Elizabeth watched as Suzanne, the art counselor, bent down and tugged lightly on the girl's pigtails. "Don't listen to that silly boy, Maggie," she said warmly. "Your mommy loves you a lot."

"How do you know?" the younger girl said between sniffles, turning her face up to the older girl.

"Because she gave you this wonderful video camera to make a movie to show her when you get home," Suzanne said, gesturing to the leather case she was carrying on her shoulder. "She loves you so much, she doesn't want to miss a minute of your summer."

The little girl seemed satisfied with that reasoning. She picked herself off the ground.

Elizabeth couldn't believe it. A video camera? For an eight-year-old? She knew that this camp catered to a privileged crowd, but she couldn't believe that some parent would trust this young a child with a video camera. Or that it was appropriate. *Ours is not to question why,* Elizabeth thought, chuckling to herself.

65

"Dwight's got cooties! Dwight's got cooties!" a little girl with long red hair chirped merrily. Suddenly all the children swarmed into chaos.

"Children! Calm down!" Suzanne shouted, clearly trying to remain calm herself. "Let's get inside so we can get our cabin assignments." But the kids continued to shriek and run in circles.

"There are treats inside," Suzanne cajoled. "Cake, cookies, soda." That did it. The group trotted inside the main lodge.

Elizabeth sat back down on the couch. *Maybe this challenge will do Jess some good,* she figured. *She's never been the most patient person. This month should give her a good dose of practice in that department.*

"Well, this is it," Jessica said to Lila at the door of the mess hall. It was the moment of truth, when all the JCs would meet the little charges.

"Are you ready?" Lila asked.

"Sure," Jessica said. But she didn't feel ready. She had an overwhelming fear that the girls would hate her on sight. *Considering my experience with children, they'll probably turn out to be six miniature witches,* Jessica thought. *Wicked witches.*

The large room had about a dozen rows of tables, with an aisle down the middle. All the girls were sitting at tables on one side, boys on the other. In the sea of squirming children Jessica spotted a sign identifying the seven- and eight-year-olds. She noticed with distress that Lacey herself was sitting with them.

"There's my table," she said with dread. "I get to be under the watchful eye of Lacey Cavannah."

"Poor you," Lila sympathized. She pointed to a table at the back of the room. "There's my table."

"Let's go," Jessica said. She took a deep breath and they both headed off for their respective tables.

"Girls, this is Jessica Wakefield, your junior counselor," Lacey announced when Jessica reached the table. "Have a seat, Jessica."

An adorable little girl with huge brown eyes and dark corkscrew curls caught Jessica's eye first. Jessica sat down at the empty spot next to her. "What's your name?" Jessica asked the girl.

"My name's Sofia. With a *f*," the girl said softly.

The girl sitting next to her gave her a small shove. "*An f*, not *a f*," she corrected. This girl looked like a slightly older version of Sofia, except that she had blue eyes. "My name's Anastasia. We're sisters. I'm older," she said to Jessica as she wrapped her arms possessively around Sofia.

Sofia squirmed out of Anastasia's arms. "Don't," she whined. Jessica smiled. They were really cute.

"What's your name again?" a girl with brown pigtails asked Jessica.

"My name is Jessica, but you can call me Jess if you'd like," Jessica answered.

67

"Jess. That's pwetty," said a girl with frizzy red hair and a gap where her two front teeth should have been.

"What's your name?" Jessica asked.

"Stephanie."

"I wish my name was Jess," another girl announced. "My name's Tanya. Do you like grilled cheese?" she asked Jessica.

Jessica smiled. "I love grilled cheese!"

Tanya held out her plate toward Jessica. "You can have mine."

"Don't you like it?" Jessica asked.

"Yes, but you can have it. I want you to have it," Tanya said.

Jessica shrugged and took the plate. "If you insist." Jessica looked over at Lacey.

Lacey nodded her approval and gestured to the girl with brown pigtails. "Jessica, this is Maggie. And this is Sarah," she said, pointing to a cute Asian-American girl whose face was framed in black bangs. Her black hair hung just below her shoulders.

"Hi," Sarah said in a small voice.

"Nice to meet you both," Jessica said.

Sofia turned her angelic face up to Jessica. "Can I sit next to you at dinner, too?"

Jessica patted Sofia on the head. "I don't see why not," she said.

"No, I want to," Anastasia said.

68

"No, I want to," Tanya said.

Lacey put up a hand. "Girls, girls, I'm sure you'll all get a chance to sit with Jessica." Lacey looked across the table at Jessica, smiling warmly.

Jessica smiled back proudly. *They actually like me*, Jessica said to herself. *Not only that—I like them!* She couldn't believe her good luck.

"Everybody say hello to Elizabeth," Rose Schwartz, the sailing counselor, said to the group of girls sitting around her at one of the tables in the mess hall. "Elizabeth, welcome to the land of ten-year-olds. This is Jennifer, Aimee, Helen, Adrienne, Emily, and Ashley," Rose said with a nod to each of the girls.

"Hi, everyone," Elizabeth said, hurrying to take a seat right beside Rose. She had been back in the cabin on her bunk, trying to come up with a plot for the camp play. Then she had noticed that noon had already come and gone. She was late for her first meeting with her campers!

Adrienne turned her light green eyes up to Rose. "Why is she so late?" she asked.

Aimee looked directly at Elizabeth. "Why are you so late?" she demanded.

"Yeah, why are you so late?" Helen echoed, pushing her huge tortoiseshell glasses up her nose.

But before Elizabeth could answer, the children erupted into a chorus of questions.

69

"Did you get lost?" Emily asked.

"Did you forget?" Ashley asked.

"Did you stop by the kitchen to bring us some sodas?" Jennifer asked, holding up her empty cup. Her fingers and face were smudged with orange cheese.

"Kids, kids, let's give her a chance to say something," Rose broke in. "Elizabeth, why were you late?"

Rose's face looked friendly, but Elizabeth thought she detected a note of disapproval. Elizabeth hoped she was just being paranoid. "I—uh—" Elizabeth stammered. "I was helping the drama coach and I lost track of time," she murmured. Hearing her pathetic attempt at a lie, Elizabeth suddenly wished she had a little of Jessica's skill at lying on demand.

"I see," Rose said. "You were helping the drama coach. Well, that's understandable, isn't it, kids?" she said brightly to the girls. Then she gave Elizabeth a meaningful stare.

Now Elizabeth knew that she wasn't being paranoid. *I'd better figure out a way to redeem myself and fast,* she told herself.

"Lizzie! Lizzie! Do you like seafood?" the little girl named Jennifer shouted. Elizabeth looked up to see Jennifer's mouth wide open, revealing a disgusting mass of chewed-up grilled cheese sandwich. "See food!" she screamed.

Elizabeth gasped. "That's disgusting!"

Jennifer just giggled, and the other girls laughed and started opening their own mouths to reveal their contents.

"Jennifer! Girls!" Rose scolded. "Playing 'seafood' is not allowed here at Camp Echo Mountain. Anyone who plays automatically doesn't get dessert all week." Chastised, the girls all looked into their laps.

"My name's Elizabeth," Elizabeth said, trying to regain some respect from the girls. "You can call me Liz if Elizabeth's too long, but I don't really like to be called Lizzie."

The girls exchanged smirks.

"Elizabeth's a prissy name," Ashley said with a quick shake of her platinum blond hair.

Aimee set her jaw firmly. "I like Lizzie better," she announced.

"Me too—I like Lizzie better," Helen echoed.

"Lizzie rhymes with dizzy!" Adrienne squealed. "Dizzy Lizzie! Dizzy Lizzie!"

"We're going to call you Dizzy Lizzie," Aimee proclaimed, giving Elizabeth a look of defiant challenge.

Elizabeth opened her mouth to protest, but she didn't know what to say. And Rose wasn't coming to her rescue this time. Elizabeth's first meeting with her campers had started out badly and had gotten worse by the minute. How could she make these kids respect her now?

What a way to start the month, Elizabeth thought woefully.

"Put your arms straight out to your sides, spacing yourselves an arm's length apart," Jessica said, lifting her own long arms horizontal with the floor. She watched as twelve little arms stuck out to form a bumpy line in front of her.

"Now lower your arms," she said. But when she didn't lower her own arms right away, the girl named Tanya kept her arms raised, dropping them only after Jessica had dropped hers.

This is kind of fun, Jessica realized. She had been dreading this, the first day of workshops. Especially after Lacey had informed her at lunch that the dance counselor with whom Jessica was supposed to have worked hadn't been able to come. Supposedly the counselor was suffering from a terrible case of bronchitis and Lacey was searching for a replacement. To make Jessica's life easier, Lacey had added a tumbling instructor named Derek Sandler. She had explained that most boys didn't want to take dance, so they would take tumbling instead. And any girl had the option of taking tumbling, too.

Now Jessica looked at the six little girls standing in a line in front of her. The girls gazed at Jessica's reflection in the floor-to-ceiling mirror, enraptured, twelve eyes following her every move.

If Jessica had been a little worried before, the feeling was long gone. After the girls' stellar behavior at lunch and their reverent obedience now, Jessica was bursting with confidence. If anyone could get a ragamuffin group like this one to learn some dance steps, Jessica Wakefield could.

"Now don't move for a minute but watch me closely," Jessica instructed. "Then you'll get a chance to copy what I do." Jessica performed a simple set of dance steps, ending with a 360-degree turn. The girls broke into wild applause and Jessica curtsied.

A little freckle-faced girl with matted brown pigtails started waving her arms wildly. Jessica didn't remember what her name was.

"Yes?" Jessica asked. "What is it?"

"Can I make a tape of you? My mommy gave me a video machine to make a movie of all the best things about camp. And you're the best thing I've seen all day."

Jessica smiled, flattered by the girl's obvious adoration. "As long as you learn the dance steps, I don't see any harm in that," she said. "What's your name again?"

"Maggie," the girl said proudly. She ran over to a chair and grabbed a video camera.

"Do you need some help running that thing?" Jessica asked, even though she herself didn't have a clue how to work it.

73

"No, I know how. My mommy taught me," Maggie said. And even though the camera looked like it weighed as much as the little girl, Maggie expertly filmed the whole workshop. With a camera rolling, Jessica the showperson came out, and she conducted the rest of her lesson with her flashiest smiles and prettiest postures.

By the end of the ninety-minute workshop Jessica noticed that the girls hadn't stopped copying her—her moves, her walk, the way she flipped her hair. They were obviously modeling themselves after her. *Pretty smart, these little kids,* Jessica thought.

Elizabeth trudged along the path from the lake toward the girls' cabins, nearly tripping with exhaustion. She had spent the whole afternoon lugging buckets and ropes back and forth between Lacey's Ford Bronco, the dock, and the boathouse.

And the girls had officially christened her Dizzy Lizzie—Diz for short. They even introduced her as Dizzy Lizzie to the boy campers who had joined them for the sailing lesson. *Pretty soon the whole camp will be calling me Dizzy Lizzie,* Elizabeth thought.

Elizabeth couldn't wait to collapse on her bunk for some peace and quiet. *Maybe I'll start a letter to Todd,* she thought. *He always has a soothing effect on me.*

But when Elizabeth got closer to the cabin, she heard a commotion inside.

Elizabeth walked in to see Nicole sitting on her bed, surrounded by Maria and Angela. Maria's arms were circled around Nicole's heaving shoulders, and Angela was patting her leg.

"I just can't believe that anyone here would have the nerve to take my diary," Nicole said between sobs.

Elizabeth caught Jessica's eye across the cabin, but Jessica only shrugged.

Nicole looked up and narrowed her eyes. "Oh, there you are," she said, her eyes fixed on Elizabeth.

"Yeah, I'm here," Elizabeth said. "Aren't I allowed to be in my own cabin?"

Nicole smirked. "Well, I didn't want to make a big deal out of it, but I saw you rummaging around in my trunk in here earlier when you thought there was no one around. And now my diary's missing."

Elizabeth's jaw dropped. "I wasn't anywhere near your trunk!" she blurted, furious that Nicole would accuse her of stealing a diary. If anyone respected the sanctity of a diary, it was Elizabeth. "I was sitting on my bed, trying to do some writing, since you kicked me off the desk!"

"You don't have to get all defensive," Nicole said. "I'm just saying what I think I saw."

Elizabeth jammed her hands on her hips.

"Well, then you're wrong about what you think you saw. Or you're *lying*," she hissed.

Jessica walked over and touched Elizabeth's arm. "Liz," she said softly. "You know you didn't take her diary, so there's no need to throw accusations back and forth."

Elizabeth looked Nicole straight in the eye. "I didn't take your diary," she said firmly.

"So you won't mind if we take a look around your area?" Angela asked.

Now she's got Angela on her side? Elizabeth wondered with dismay. "Go right ahead," she said confidently.

Wordlessly Angela went over to Elizabeth's bunk and began inspecting her belongings. After a moment she held up a small blue book. "I found this under your mattress, Liz. Is it yours?" she asked.

"That's my diary!" Nicole shouted.

Elizabeth gasped. "I have no idea how that got under my mattress! I absolutely, positively had nothing to do with it!" she screamed.

Nicole just smiled sweetly. "I'm sure it was a mistake," she said. "Maybe one of the campers put it there as a prank."

I've been set up! Elizabeth realized. She looked at Maria, but Maria wouldn't look at her. Then Elizabeth recalled Nicole's words of the night before: *Maria's my friend.*

Elizabeth shivered. Score one round for Nicole.

Chapter 5

Lila bolted awake to the sound of a bugle. *Where am I?* she wondered for a second. Then she remembered. *Camp Echo Hell,* she grumbled to herself, stuffing her head under her pillow.

Lila was exhausted after only two days with the campers. Her thirteen-year-olds were turning out to be a serious handful. The Sulky Six, as Lila had started to call them, complained about being too old for nearly every activity. *As if they're not immature little children themselves,* Lila thought every time they whined about finger painting or flag ceremonies or camp songs. She couldn't even count how many times she'd heard the words "how childish" in the last two days.

Tiffany was the worst, in Lila's opinion. She was blond, tall, and skinny and had the longest eyelashes Lila had ever seen. If she didn't have such an unattractive personality, Lila might have considered her pretty—for a thirteen-year-old. But Tiffany was an obnoxious spoiled brat who kept talking about how as soon as she got her braces off, her mother was going to take her to New York to become a famous model. She never just said *model*—always *famous model*.

Tiffany also thought she was a fashion expert. The first thing Tiffany had said to Lila on meeting her was, "Isn't pastel pink lipstick last year's look? *This* year the look is muted colors."

"Pastels are always in," Lila had retorted. "But for someone as blond as you, I can see why you might have trouble."

Tiffany had just sulked.

Tiffany and her best friend, Amber, had been coming to Camp Echo Mountain for seven years. Amber was almost as obnoxious as Tiffany, but Amber was a little pudgy, so she didn't have ambitions of becoming a famous model. With her porcelain skin, blue eyes, and strawberry blond hair, Lila thought that Amber would actually turn out prettier than Tiffany. She just had to lose her baby fat.

Nancy and Robin were athletic jock types. From their complaints Lila had figured out that their mothers had forced them to come to Camp Echo Mountain instead of the sports camp they wanted to attend. And Lila bore the brunt of their bitterness. While Tiffany and Amber considered Lila a fashion failure, Robin and Nancy considered her a fashion slave. Every time they talked about how shallow and vain she was, Lila would remind herself that they were just jealous of her stylish beauty. *If I had Nancy's ruddy, freckled complexion and Robin's pimply mess, I'd probably be jealous of me, too,* Lila realized.

Then there was Samantha. Samantha was a beautiful black girl who constantly reminded Lila that her high-powered family basically ran the city of Atlanta. Not only was she a snob, she fancied herself a talented artist. Every time Lila made an artistic error, like when she didn't know the difference between paste and glue, Samantha laughed the loudest.

Odette, the sixth of the Sulky Six, was Samantha's twin sister. These twins were definitely not identical—in looks or demeanor. Samantha clearly got the beauty genes, and Odette got the brains. A quiet girl, Odette was never without a paperback. Lila had even seen her reading at the campfire the night before, spilling s'mores into the pages of her book.

A terrible crew, Lila thought, burrowing under her covers. *If it weren't for the hope of getting to know Bo, I would call my dad and insist he send a plane for me.*

But the only time she'd seen Bo in the last two days had been at meals, and only from a distance.

Lila dragged herself out of bed, hoping to beat the morning scramble for positions in the bathroom. There were only three mirrors in the girls' bathroom, and with six junior counselors and six senior counselors, it was every woman for herself. Lila couldn't risk going to breakfast without first completing her morning beauty routine. The Sulky Six would notice—and so might Bo.

Lila was the first one in the cabin to stumble outside. "They're awake!" she heard someone yell. She rubbed her eyes to see the small picnic area humming with activity.

Jessica came up behind Lila in the doorway. "What the—?" she asked.

"We thought we'd surprise you girls with a pancake breakfast right outside your door," Rose said with a smile. Right next to her stood Maggie, her video camera rolling.

"Are you surprised?" Maggie asked, pointing the camera at Jessica and Lila.

"Yes, Maggie, we're surprised," Jessica said sleepily.

Lila just groaned. She saw that her girls were sulking at a table by themselves. *At least they look as tired as I feel,* she thought.

Then Lila spotted Bo loading up on pancakes and bacon. He didn't seem to be heading toward anyone with his plate. *Forget my campers,* Lila crowed to herself. *I'm having breakfast with Bo!*

She pushed past Rose and Maggie and made a beeline toward him. Then she stopped. *I haven't even showered,* she remembered. But watching Bo wolf down his pancakes, Lila realized she didn't have time. *Bo just better be one of those guys who actually likes the natural look,* Lila said to herself as she marched toward him.

From her bed Elizabeth had listened as the other girls stumbled around the cabin, getting ready to head for the showers. Only Elizabeth knew that they were heading for a rude awakening: the surprise pancake breakfast right outside their cabin that the senior counselors had planned. Bernard, the head cook, had told her about the surprise the night before when he had found her sitting in the mess hall in the middle of the night.

Elizabeth had been trying to work on the play, and she only had peace and quiet when everyone else was asleep. Also, since Nicole didn't know Elizabeth had already started writing, she was giving herself a head start. Not that it had done any good so far. Elizabeth still hadn't come up with a good subject.

Now she rolled over in her bed, putting off the inevitable. She dreaded this breakfast. Her girls were bad enough when they were alone; they were impossible in group settings.

"Dizzy Lizzie! Where's Dizzy Lizzie?" Elizabeth heard someone outside scream. It sounded like Aimee, the girl who had first christened her with the nickname.

A chant started. "Diz! Diz! We want Diz!" It gained momentum. "Diz! Diz! We want *Diz!*" Elizabeth had no choice but to get up and go out there or the brats would never shut up.

She rolled out of bed and dragged a comb through her hair, fastening it back into a ponytail. Then she thought better of it, twisting her hair up into a tight bun. The girls had taken a liking to pulling her hair, and it was better to keep it pinned close to her scalp. She took a deep breath and headed for the door. Time to face the music.

"There she is!" screamed Helen, Aimee's best friend.

"Good morning, girls," Elizabeth said, trying to smile.

The girls swarmed around her. "You sure look ugly in the morning," Emily said with a toss of her honey blond hair.

Jennifer pulled a wet clump of hair out of her mouth. "You look like you slept in a sewer," she added.

Elizabeth tried to keep her head up as she walked to the food table to pick up a tray.

The girls followed. "Is that a mosquito bite on the end of your nose?" Adrienne asked.

"No, it's a big red wart!" Aimee announced. The girls howled with laughter. "Diz has a wart! Diz has a wart!" they chanted.

Elizabeth knew she should have stayed in bed.

"Do you like to go hiking?" Lila asked Bo. With his rugged good looks, he seemed to be a real mountain man.

"Do I like to hike? You mean like taking little walks through the wilderness, watching birds and looking at nature?"

"Um, yeah, I guess so." Lila nodded.

Bo scoffed. "Hikes are for wimps," he said with a dismissive wave of the hand.

Lila frowned, hurt by his snub.

Bo seemed to notice. "I mean, hiking's okay," he added quickly. "I take lots of hikes. It's just that I'd rather do more exciting stuff—mountain climbing, rock climbing, mountain biking. You know, stuff that really makes the heart pound. Danger's a rush."

Lila nodded, trying to convey enthusiasm about these activities, which were as foreign to her as doing the dishes at home. "What's the most exciting thing you've ever done?" she asked.

Bo looked at her blankly, then snapped his fingers as if struck by a memory. "This one time I went kayaking down the Colorado River after one of the wettest winters ever. They had never seen the river so high. The rapids were wicked," Bo retold with drama. "Everyone was capsizing right and left, and I just knew I was going to eat it."

"Did you?" Lila asked, taking a dainty bite of her pancakes. "Oh, boy, did I!" Bo said with a casual laugh. "I was heading down this really hairy part when my kayak flipped over and I got trapped under water. I couldn't unhook the safety belt around my waist. I was sure I was going to drown."

Bo shook his head. "Lucky for me I had a pocket knife. I sawed right through the safety strap and just barely made it to the surface before I ran out of air."

Lila nodded, impressed. But something about his story didn't quite sit right. *I didn't know they strapped you into kayaks. Don't they flip over all the time?* she wondered. Then she pushed the doubt out of her mind. *After all, what do I know about kayaking?*

Bo started in on another story. "And this other time I was hang gliding in the Mojave Desert when I hit a wind pocket and started losing altitude really fast."

Lila gasped. "What did you do?"

"Luckily I'd been fully trained in crash landings, so I wasn't hurt too badly. Just a sprained ankle," Bo said, raising up his leg to show Lila his tanned, golden-haired ankle. Then he stuffed pancakes into his mouth, smiling at Lila as he chewed.

Lila smiled back at him. *How can someone so strong and manly also look so absolutely sweet and adorable?* Lila wondered.

But as Lila listened to him rattle off one daring hobby after another, she felt her heart sink. She hated all those activities. Lila thought back to how worried she'd been that Bo would see her without makeup and chuckled to herself. *Bo definitely seems to be one of those guys who likes the natural look,* she realized. *Maybe a bit too much.*

What would Bo say if he saw me as I usually look—perfectly put together in the most expensive makeup and clothes? Lila wondered. *Or if he knew that the closest I ever get to the great outdoors is the manicured gardens of Fowler Crest?*

Lila knew what he'd say. He'd say, "See ya."

But she had promised herself to do whatever it took to get him. So if Bo liked gutsy girls, she would be the gutsiest girl he had ever met.

"You won't believe the harrowing ordeal I had in Death Valley last spring," Lila blurted. She proceeded to recount Jessica's experience as if it were her own. *Jess won't mind me borrowing her story since it's for a good cause,* Lila figured.

When Lila had finished her story, Bo exclaimed, "I can't believe you almost got killed by escaped convicts!"

Lila poured more syrup on her pancakes. "Yeah, well, now it feels like the whole thing happened to someone else," she said breezily.

Bo nodded. "I know what you mean. That happens to me after I go through something totally mind blowing, too," he said, looking at Lila with admiration.

Since Bo seemed to be so impressed with her bravery, Lila invented a new story about a mountain-climbing adventure. "We camped above the tree line and I was the only one who didn't get altitude sickness," she relayed. "In fact, the farther I am from civilization, the better I feel."

"I know," Bo agreed. "Isn't it the most liberating thing to feel like you're totally vulnerable to the wilds of nature?"

Lila smiled, hoping he didn't notice the horror in her eyes. This line of conversation had gone far enough for the moment. Lila needed to change the subject before Bo realized how much she was lying. She looked around the picnic area and noticed Elizabeth's campers running wild.

"Poor Liz," Lila said with feeling. "I wish there were something I could do to help her." Lila wished nothing of the sort, but she knew that guys loved girls who were sympathetic and caring.

Bo looked around. "Who's Liz?"

Lila gestured to Elizabeth, who was trying to coax the girls to a table. "The blond over there with the band of screaming monkeys."

"Oh, *Liz*," Bo said. "I'd been wondering why a parent would name their kid Diz. That's what I heard the other kids call her."

Lila couldn't help but giggle. It was truly fun to see the usually perfect Elizabeth Wakefield going down in flames.

Bo looked at his wristwatch and jumped up. "Gotta go! I have flag-raising duties today!" he said. Then he stopped and locked eyes with Lila. Putting one hand on the table, he leaned over. "I think it's great how we have so much in common," Bo whispered in her ear.

Lila gazed up into his eyes. "We do, don't we?" she whispered back.

Bo kissed her lightly on the cheek. Lila felt a shiver run from her cheek all the way through her body to her toes.

There was no doubt about it. Lila was in love.

"It's a beautiful day at Camp Echo Mountain! It's a beautiful day at Camp Echo Mountain!" Aaron, Bo, Buford, and Johansen chanted as they walked in formation, carrying the American flag between them as gently as if it were an egg. When they reached the base of the flagpole, the boys carefully unfolded the flag and attached it to the ropes.

All the campers and counselors stood in a large circle around the flagpole, watching in silence as the flag began its ascent.

All except for Elizabeth's six young campers. They wouldn't stop squirming and fidgeting.

"Diz!" Adrienne whined.

Elizabeth put a finger to her lips. "Shhh!"

Adrienne fiddled with the three small wire hoops she wore on one ear. "But Ashley was pulling on my earrings!"

Ashley narrowed her charcoal gray eyes. "Adrienne hit me first."

"Did you hit Ashley?" Elizabeth whispered to Adrienne.

Maria glared at Elizabeth from where she was

standing with her campers a few feet away. "Shhh!" she hissed.

What can I do? Elizabeth asked silently with her eyes.

Maria just shrugged and looked away.

"I saw the whole thing! I saw the whole thing!" Jennifer sang out. Her voice disrupted the silence of the ritual.

The flag jerked to a stop as the four boys stopped pulling to check out the source of the commotion.

"Elizabeth!" Lacey barked. "Please get your girls under control!"

"Sorry," Elizabeth said in a small voice. She felt the glares of everyone on her as the flag resumed its ascent.

"Now everyone raise your hand to your heart and join together to say the pledge of allegiance," Lacey instructed after the flag was raised.

"Your right hand, not your left hand! Cover your heart with your *right* hand," Elizabeth hissed to her girls. Not one of them had gotten it right. "I pledge allegiance . . ." Elizabeth recited.

Jennifer tugged at Elizabeth's shorts. "Dizzy Lizzie, I don't feel so good. Can I go to the bathroom?"

"After the flag-raising ceremony," Elizabeth whispered. ". . . and to the republic . . ."

Suddenly Jennifer collapsed to the ground and proceeded to throw up her pancakes.

Chapter 6

"I don't want to go to awts and cwafts," Stephanie announced after the flag-raising ceremony. "My sister Tiffany said the awts and cwafts counselor is mean."

Jessica smiled. "She did, did she? The younger arts and crafts counselor or the older one?" she asked, even though she already knew the answer.

"The younger one," Stephanie said, pushing her tongue through the gap in her teeth.

Jessica laughed. "I shouldn't laugh," she told Stephanie. "Lila's my best friend." But a part of Jessica admired Lila for refusing to soften her snobby personality for anyone—not even a thirteen-year-old. *Except Bo,* Jessica amended silently. Lila had really gone off the deep end this time, pretending to be outdoorsy. *When is she finally going to figure out that trying to be something you're not never works?* Jessica bit her lip, suddenly remembering all the guys she had met—and dated—by putting on a role. *But that's different,* she decided. *That's acting.*

Tanya pulled on Jessica's shorts. "Jessica, can't we please stay with you all day today? We don't want to be with anyone else."

"We could help you teach the other girls," Anastasia offered.

Little Sofia didn't say anything but clutched Jessica's hand tightly.

Jessica sighed. She had been enjoying the adulation of her young charges, but by now she was starting to feel a bit stifled. Whenever she was with them, Jessica couldn't do anything, say anything, or go anywhere without six little girls copying her every move. It was getting on her nerves. She had even developed a name for them: the Wannabees.

And little Maggie insisted on taping everything. Jessica had to constantly watch what she did because Maggie had a knack for being there with her camera at the worst possible time—like that morning at breakfast when Jessica had inadvertently spilled some syrup on her chin. Maggie had caught the embarrassing moment on tape before Jessica could wipe away the unsightly dribble.

Even the fact that Jessica was scheduled to teach dance to Lila's Surly Six today didn't seem all that unattractive after two days with the Wannabees.

Jessica smiled down at the girls. "Well, I can't change the rules. Anyway, I think you girls will like arts and crafts." Jessica crouched down to Sofia's eye level. "Don't you like finger painting?"

"I like to be with you," Sofia answered.

Jessica groaned.

Half an hour later Jessica longed for the Wannabees. At least they listened to her and followed her orders. Lila's group of insolent adolescents griped about everything. The only activity they seemed to enjoy was waterskiing and the "cool waterskiing JC from New York." *How perfect that the only girl they seem to like is Nicole, one of the nastiest girls I've ever met,* Jessica said to herself.

But what really annoyed Jessica was how the girls second-guessed her every step.

"Do you want to give us an injury?" Tiffany asked when Jessica told them to jog in place for a couple of minutes to warm up. "We need to stretch out before we do anything."

"I thought dance teachers were supposed to know something about fitness," Amber added with a sneer.

Nancy jumped in. "Give me a break," she scoffed. "What would a cheerleader know about fitness? All cheerleaders do is stand around and look pretty."

"Pretty and easy," Robin said with a smirk.

That did it. Jessica had had enough. "Cheerleaders

think it's really funny how the only girls who criticize us for the way we look are the girls who couldn't get on a cheerleading squad if they *paid* for the privilege," she told Robin.

Robin and Nancy just stood with their mouths open in shock. Tiffany and Amber snickered.

"That's not a very mature attitude, young lady," Samantha said haughtily.

Jessica looked at Samantha in disbelief. *Mature attitude? Who is she to talk? And who is she to call me a young lady?* But Jessica decided to let it go— Lila had warned her about Samantha's formidable tantrums. "Robin, Nancy, I'm sorry for that childish insult, but when in Rome . . ." Jessica said, trailing off. She wondered whether the girls would pick up on her dig.

Odette, who had refused to participate and was sitting quietly in the corner, looked up from her book. She smiled at Jessica.

Somebody's on the ball, Jessica thought, smiling back at Odette. "Anyway, for your information, the safest way to work out is to do a light warm-up to get the blood moving through your muscles, then you stretch. You can do serious harm to your body if you try to stretch out muscles that are cold," she said with authority. The girls were silenced.

"Very well put," came a voice from the door. It was Lacey.

Jessica smiled. *Scoring some more points with*

the big boss, she congratulated herself.

"Jessica, can I speak with you for a minute?" Lacey asked.

As the girls erupted into a chorus of "Ooooohs" Jessica felt her stomach lurch. Had Lacey heard her caustic remark about Robin and Nancy?

"Wipe that look of worry off your face," Lacey said when they stepped outside. "I've been extremely impressed with the way you've handled yourself. Especially since you're all on your own," she added sincerely.

I guess she must have missed my outburst, Jessica thought with relief. "Thank you, Lacey. That means a lot, coming from you," she said. She knew she was kissing up, but Lacey seemed like the kind of woman who would fall for flattery. And from the smile that broke out on Lacey's face, Jessica knew she'd guessed correctly.

"That's very nice of you to say, Jessica," Lacey said, stroking Jessica's cheek in a motherly fashion. Then she frowned. "I have some good news and some bad news. Which do you want to hear first?"

"Um, the bad news."

"Well, the young woman I found to take over as dance instructor just took a job with a summer program in New York. I'm afraid at this point it will be nearly impossible to find a replacement. Do you think you can manage on your own for the rest of the month?"

Jessica didn't know what to say. She thought she could manage. But then again, she hadn't yet had the pleasure of teaching Elizabeth's troublesome group, and she didn't look forward to facing that experience by herself.

Lacey continued, "Because we could just cancel dance workshops and have all the campers take tumbling. With your skills you could be a real help to Derek."

"That's true," Jessica thoughtfully. *That would be the easiest thing to do, but I don't want to do it,* she realized. She liked being in charge. "Why don't I teach dance to the girls who'd get the most out of it?" she suggested. "Like the youngest girls."

"That's fine," Lacey said. "Whatever you think is best. I have confidence in your judgment."

Jessica smiled. *Lacey's a smart woman,* she said to herself. "What about the good news?"

"Well," Lacey started. Then she leaned closer to Jessica. "I know that these girls aren't the easiest to deal with," she said in a hushed tone. "So I've asked Derek to come help you with them today." Lacey turned around. "And there he is now," she said, waving to a tall, muscular boy who was walking toward the building.

Jessica gasped. Derek was blond and tan, and he had clear blue eyes—exactly like Ken Matthews, her ex-boyfriend. The resemblance was unnerving.

94

Derek's face lit up in a friendly smile. "Great to meet you, Jessica."

"Um . . . hi."

"Well, I'll leave you two to your workshop," Lacey said with a knowing smile.

After Lacey had walked away, Derek leaned closer to Jessica. "Lacey didn't tell me how gorgeous you were," he whispered flirtatiously.

"Thanks," Jessica mumbled, still in shock over Derek's uncanny resemblance to Ken.

Suddenly Samantha appeared in the doorway. "Young lady!" she snapped. "Quit your flirting and get back to work!"

"Did you have a good day today?" Elizabeth asked, handing a shovel to Maria. The two of them had been assigned the after-dinner duty of clearing the campfire area of ashes and debris.

"It was a pretty good day," Maria answered in a flat voice.

"That pancake breakfast this morning sure was a rude awakening, wasn't it?" Elizabeth asked, trying to get the conversation going.

"I guess," Maria answered.

Elizabeth tried to remain bright in the face of Maria's coolness. *I hope I'm just imagining things,* Elizabeth thought. But ever since the episode with Nicole's stolen diary, Maria had seemed distant. Elizabeth swept ashes from the center of the campfire into a small pail. "The weather today sure was fabulous," she said. *I can't believe I'm reduced to talking about the weather,* Elizabeth said to herself. *Maria and I used to have dozens of things to talk about.*

"It was nice," Maria admitted as she filled a garbage bag with empty marshmallow wrappers and sticky roasting sticks.

"The air up here is so much cleaner and fresher than back home," Elizabeth said. "Even though Sweet Valley is close to the ocean, the air quality doesn't come close to that of this mountain air." Elizabeth felt herself babbling, but Maria's unresponsiveness was spurring her to fill the silence. "How are your workshops going?" she asked.

"Pretty well. Joey is a really good teacher."

"Is he?" Elizabeth asked in a high-pitched voice. She hoped it didn't betray her excitement on hearing his name. "What kinds of things does he do?"

"He has an excellent rapport with the kids. They really seem to respect him," Maria said.

"That's great," Elizabeth said, feeling awkward. *I wish the same thing could be said about me,* she thought gloomily. She wondered whether Maria was making an indirect comment about her own lack of rapport with her kids. At every group function Elizabeth's girls were the absolute worst, humiliating her constantly with the whole camp watching.

And the sailing classes with Rose weren't turning out much better. All the campers now called her Dizzy Lizzie or Diz, and with her repeated public embarrassments by her six brats none of the campers gave her much respect. In addition, she was turning out to be a terrible sailor, constantly getting confused between the stern and the bow.

To make matters worse, Nicole was the water-skiing JC, so Elizabeth had to see her at the lake all day, every day. And Nicole was a dynamite water-skier—she could ski on one leg and backward, do jumps and flips, and perform dramatic combinations. Nicole also always managed to do her most daring stunts a little bit too close to the sailboat area, rocking Elizabeth's boat in the process. All the campers seemed to think Nicole was cool.

The only positive thing about seeing Nicole all the time was that Elizabeth knew Nicole wasn't doing any writing on the play. *Not that the time I'm spending awake at night is doing me any good,* Elizabeth reminded herself. All the pressure she was feeling, along with her constant state of fatigue, didn't exactly help to spur her creative juices.

Elizabeth wanted nothing more than to reveal her insecurities—about the play, about Nicole, about her naughty campers—to Maria. But she knew she couldn't. Maria didn't seem to be her friend. They went about their cleanup without saying more than an occasional "Excuse me" or "Can you hand me that garbage bag?" The silence between them was almost painful. Elizabeth couldn't wait to finish.

Suddenly Joey appeared from the darkness. "Time to get the fire going," he said. He was carrying a large canvas bag stuffed with firewood.

Startled, Elizabeth dropped her broom at the sound of his voice. She had been so focused on getting her job done that she hadn't heard anyone coming.

"Sorry, didn't mean to startle you," he said, lowering the wood to the ground.

"That's OK," Elizabeth said. Her heart didn't slow down. "I was just lost in a daydream."

"Are you thinking about the camp play? Maria tells me you're a talented writer."

Elizabeth looked at Maria and thought she detected a small smile before Maria cast down her eyes. "Yeah, I've been working on it," Elizabeth said weakly.

"You want to tell me about it?" Joey asked.

Elizabeth, entranced by the way the stubble on Joey's chin sparkled in the moonlight, didn't know what to say. She couldn't tell him she was at a total loss for ideas. "I can't reveal anything until it's finished," she said mysteriously.

"Fair enough," Joey replied. He looked from Elizabeth to Maria. "You two sure look like you could use a cleanup before the campfire."

Maria looked down at herself. "Soot has a way of sticking to everything," she said with a laugh.

Joey laughed along. "I think I've got everything under control here. You're free to go."

But as Maria gathered her things and headed toward the showers, Elizabeth stood frozen. She didn't want to move; she wanted to stay right there and watch as Joey piled up the wood.

There was no doubt about it. Elizabeth had a huge crush.

"Now that we've had three days to get to know each other, I thought it was high time you all learned the camp legend," Lacey said in her slow southern drawl. Everyone was gathered around the huge fire that Joey had built. Everyone except Maggie, who was scurrying around the crowd, video camera in hand.

"Does she ever stop?" Elizabeth whispered to Jessica, who was sitting on the ground next to her.

"Never!" Jessica whispered back. "I wish Lacey would do something about that girl."

But Lacey didn't even seem to notice Maggie as she launched into her story. "Many years ago when my husband, Mr. Cavannah, was still alive, there was a young man who lived in the woods of Echo Mountain. Every morning you could hear the sound of him chopping wood all across the lake. He was a strange fellow, living off nature and such.

99

But he seemed harmless, so Mr. Cavannah and I hired him to do odd jobs for us here at the camp— building and fixing things and so forth."

The fire cracked and popped as Lacey continued. "Anyway, one night I was taking a walk by the lake and I heard some noises coming from the boathouse. I went to the doorway and shone my flashlight inside." Lacey's eyes opened wide with horror. "There, in plain view, were the woodsman and my head counselor . . . together!" Lacey paused, letting the expression of disgust on her face tell the rest of the story.

Elizabeth heard titters from around the campfire.

Lacey put her hands on her hips. "You may think that's humorous, but I'll have you know, as long as this camp is in the Cavannah family, camp counselors will know better than to engage in such behavior," she said, pointing a long index finger at their faces.

The tittering stopped, and Lacey continued. "I dismissed the girl immediately back to her cabin and ordered the wanton woodsman never to come back to Camp Echo Mountain," Lacey relayed. "They cried and carried on about how they couldn't live without each other. But I was having none of it. They had disobeyed my rules." Again she glared menacingly at the group circled around her.

"Well, the silly girl wouldn't eat, sleep, or talk," Lacey explained. "Her counselor friends, her campers—even Bernard the cook, who had taken a special liking to her—couldn't do anything to bring her out of her stupor." Lacey shook her head at the memory.

She let out a loud sigh. "After two days of this ridiculous behavior, we woke up one morning to find the girl's bunk empty. We searched high and low through the camp, but she was nowhere to be found. The strange thing was, all her belongings remained behind—even her snapshots from home."

Lacey shook her head again. "We had no choice but to call the police, even though it brought a good deal of unwanted attention to the camp. The police searched through the woods for hours until they finally found the ramshackle log cabin the woodsman called home."

Lacey lowered her voice almost to a whisper. "The cabin was deserted. And again, all the belongings were left behind. There was even a bowl of cold oatmeal on the table, by now collecting bugs and dust."

Elizabeth was transfixed. *What a great story!* she said to herself. *Maybe I've just found my play!*

"They had disappeared without a trace," Lacey whispered. She crossed her arms in front of her. "The girl's parents offered a reward, and the story was picked up by the national media. But the counselor and the woodsman never showed. With the arrival of fall, we had to assume that the couple had somehow died in the woods—possibly in a forest fire."

Then Lacey sat up straight and her face took on an ominous expression. "But some people still say that the couple's disappearance was not complete." She paused, then continued speaking in a hushed tone. "To this day, on nights when the air is still and the moon is dim, people report they can hear the sound of chopping wood echo across the lake."

A number of campers started whimpering with fright, but Elizabeth rolled her eyes. She had long ago stopped believing in ghost stories. *Is anyone besides the kids really buying this?* she wondered.

Then Elizabeth noticed Nicole, who was sitting next to Joey, inch closer to him and wrap her arms through his.

Nicole looked over to Elizabeth, a triumphant sparkle in her eyes.

Elizabeth glowered. "I'll get even with that hard-edged, two-faced girl if it kills me," she vowed, mumbling the words under her breath.

She looked up to see that Maggie was shooting her video camera right in Elizabeth's direction.

Chapter 7

"Do you guys want to change quickly and head down to the lake for a mini-sunbathing session?" Jessica asked Lila and Elizabeth when they met up with each other after the flag-raising ceremony on Friday morning. The campers had all been rounded up and locked away in the main lodge that morning for a nature movie. Lacey had generously excused most of the counselors and JCs from attending, granting them a precious few minutes of freedom.

"Why bother?" Elizabeth grumbled. "We'll just have to turn around and go back to work before long."

"Liz is right," Lila said. "We might as well just stay here." She plopped herself down at a picnic table.

Jessica shrugged and sat down backward on the

103

bench across from Lila, leaning back against the table. It appeared that most of the other counselors were also too exhausted to do anything more ambitious with their free time. Everyone seemed to be here in the main picnic area.

Jessica started to daydream about her dance class that afternoon. *Maybe we should do a hip-hop routine*, she thought. *Or maybe I'm in more of a jazz mood*. It was fun—Jessica could teach the girls whatever she felt like teaching them. It gave her a gratifying sense of power.

"What are you doing with those?" Elizabeth asked as Lila pulled a stack of wilderness magazines out of her backpack.

"Oh, didn't you hear?" Jessica cut in. "Lila's decided that by reading a couple of magazines, she can make Bo believe she's a wilderness freak."

Lila cocked her chin. "I just want to share interests with the man I love."

"The man you love?" Jessica asked, incredulous.

Lila arched an eyebrow. "Yes, the man I love."

"If love is real, you know it right away," Elizabeth said suddenly, her eyes misty.

Jessica stared at her sister in shock. *Now Liz is getting boy crazy, too?* "Is that how it was with Todd?" she asked, knowing full well that Elizabeth was thinking about someone else entirely.

Elizabeth looked startled. "No, I mean yes. I mean no." She stumbled over her words, then took a breath. "I mean, I think it's possible to fall in love right away, when it's right."

"Like with Joey?" Jessica taunted.

Elizabeth glared at Jessica. "I'm not in love with Joey!" she declared.

Jessica chuckled silently. *If only Liz would just admit that she has a thing for Joey,* Jessica thought. *It would be much healthier.* But considering her sister's commitment to Todd, Jessica knew Elizabeth would never even admit to herself that she had a crush on someone besides her boyfriend. Jessica decided to change the subject. "You want to hear something strange? I'm actually looking forward to my afternoon workshop."

"Are you crazy?" Elizabeth gasped. "What could you possibly be looking forward to?"

"I like being a teacher, and I like the responsibility Lacey has given me," Jessica said with pride.

Lila looked up from her magazine. "And I bet you like the cute tumbling instructor, too," Lila said with a wink.

Derek *was* cute. But he reminded Jessica too much of Ken—and she still couldn't think about Ken without remembering too many painful memories. "Li, didn't you hear me tell you over and over again that I'm not going after boys this summer?"

"Yeah, right," Lila said. "Still, you can't make

me believe that having a hot tumbling instructor isn't making your workshops a lot more fun. And there's nothing wrong with that." She looked seriously at Jessica. "A little more attention in the love department might do you some good."

Jessica groaned. "For your information, Lila, Derek won't be joining my class today. And even if he were, that wouldn't be the reason I'm looking forward to class. He's really not my type."

"Not your type? But he looks exactly like Ken!" Lila exclaimed.

Jessica looked at her friend. *Sometimes Lila can be so dense.* "Precisely," she said pointedly. Lila looked into her lap.

Elizabeth reached across the table and patted Jessica's hand. "How are you doing, Jess?" she asked in a soft voice.

Jessica gently pulled her hand out from under Elizabeth's. "Don't worry, Liz," she said. "Thanks for your concern, but I'm fine. In fact, I'm better than fine. I can't tell you how liberating it is not to think about guys."

Lila looked at Jessica as if she'd just announced she had decided to become a camel herder.

"Don't look so shocked, Li," Jessica said. "Maybe if you'd stop pining over Bo, you'd actually appreciate the cool things you're learning from Suzanne in arts and crafts."

"Give me a break," Lila mumbled. "How can I

get excited about tissue-paper flowers when I haven't spoken to Bo in three days?"

Jessica rolled her eyes.

Elizabeth smiled wanly at Jessica. "I think it's great that you're enjoying yourself, Jess," she remarked flatly.

Jessica looked at her sister. With her lackluster attitude and the deep purple circles under her eyes, Elizabeth looked severely fatigued. And she couldn't stop jerking her head over to the table where Joey and Maria were sitting together. They looked like they were going over lesson plans.

Jessica looked from Elizabeth to Lila. *My decision not to chase boys this summer was definitely a good one,* Jessica thought as she observed their unhappy faces. *I'm having the best time of the three of us by far.*

"Jessica! Is that you?"

Jessica had left Elizabeth and Lila to their gloom and was walking by the camp office when she heard Lacey calling her name through the open door.

"Did you want to see me?" she asked, poking her head into Lacey's office.

Lacey was standing behind her desk. "Come on in, Jessica. Have a seat," she said, motioning to one of the leather armchairs across from her.

Jessica sat down.

"You've probably noticed that I've been around you a good deal these past few days," Lacey said as she took her seat.

"Well, now that you mention it, you seem to drop in on my workshops more than any others," Jessica said. "Have I been doing okay?" She already knew that Lacey thought she was doing better than okay, but she also knew that a little modesty goes a long way.

"Jessica, you've been doing wonderfully." Lacey reached across her desk to pat Jessica's forearm. "I must admit, at first I was concerned how you'd fare without a senior counselor to guide you." She smiled. "But my concern has been unnecessary—you've proven yourself an able dance teacher. In fact, you seem to me to be a born leader. It's obvious that the girls look up to you." Lacey's eyes sparkled with warmth.

"Thank you, I've had a lot of fun getting to know them," Jessica said. And she meant it—she was learning that she had a way with kids after all.

Lacey continued, "Because I've been so impressed with your maturity, I would like to ask you a favor."

"What?" Jessica asked.

"We're having our first camp social on Sunday night, and I was wondering if you would be in charge of making it a fun party. I'm not giving you much time, but that kind of thing seems right up your alley."

How right you are, Jessica agreed silently. "Sure!" she replied. Camp socials could be dreary, but with Jessica Wakefield running the show, it would be the best party Camp Echo Mountain had ever seen.

Feeling on top of the world after her meeting with Lacey, Jessica hummed to herself as she walked back to the girls' side of camp. *Who knew I would turn out to be such a natural at this camp counselor thing?* Jessica thought happily.

When she passed by the bathroom, she glanced inside and did a double take. Standing in front of one of the sinks was little Tanya, her hair an orange-yellow sticky mess. Sitting on the floor was a huge bottle of hydrogen peroxide.

"Tanya! What do you think you're doing?" Jessica screamed.

Tanya turned, startled. Then her face broke into a huge grin. "You're the prettiest girl I ever met, and I want to look just like you," she said cheerfully.

Jessica groaned. "Tanya, I'm a natural blond. I don't bleach my hair to get it to look like this," she said, running her fingers through her hair.

"I don't care," Tanya said, fluffing her matted hair. "If I have to bleach my hair to look like you, that's OK."

Jessica rolled her eyes. "But with this mess, you won't look anything like me!"

Tanya's chin quivered, and her eyes welled up with tears. "You think I'm ugly!" she wailed.

Jessica frowned. She hadn't meant to insult the poor little girl. Jessica walked over to the sink and crouched down to Tanya's eye level. She took the sobbing girl's hand. "Tanya, don't cry," she cooed. "I only meant to say that your dir—" She stopped herself from saying *dirty blond.* "Your speckled blond hair works on you. You're very pretty just the way you are."

Tanya hiccuped. "Do you mean that?" she asked, her eyes wide.

Jessica stroked Tanya's cheek. "Of course I do," she answered.

Tanya threw her arms around Jessica, rubbing her sticky mess into Jessica's neck. "You're the best JC ever!" she cried.

Jessica smiled. *Another crisis diverted,* she told herself.

Then, with a start, Jessica remembered that Tanya, who lived in town, was being picked up that afternoon for a special weekend leave for her grandmother's birthday party. There wouldn't be time to fix Tanya's hair before her family arrived.

Even though she wasn't responsible for Tanya's stunt, Jessica was sure she'd be blamed. *What will her family think of me?* she wondered with dread.

"Elizabeth! Where's the extra rope I asked you to pick up from the supply shed?" Rose asked when Elizabeth walked up to the dock, a few minutes late for Friday afternoon's class.

"I'm sorry, Rose, I guess it must have slipped my mind," Elizabeth apologized.

"A lot of things seem to be slipping your mind lately," Rose snapped. "Watch the kids until I get back." With that, Rose marched up toward the supply shed, leaving Elizabeth alone with the group of eleven-year-old boys and girls.

Elizabeth turned to the twelve expectant faces seated on the dock. *Please give me a break today*, she silently implored them. Elizabeth had been dragging herself around all week, but today was the worst. The camp legend that Lacey had retold at the campfire on Tuesday night was turning out to be the ideal subject matter for the play. Elizabeth had been in the mess hall every night since then, writing furiously. And last night Elizabeth had stayed up until she heard the birds outside chirping the first sign of dawn. She was almost done.

And now she was paying for it. Up until today, Rose had been very understanding. She had seemed to believe Elizabeth's explanation for her fatigue—that she was having trouble getting used to the altitude. But Elizabeth knew Rose's patience wouldn't last much longer. Today Elizabeth had clearly pushed Rose's patience one step too far.

I need to be on my very best behavior for the

rest of the day, Elizabeth realized. She put on her most cheerful face. "Have any of you ever been in a sailboat before?" she asked the group seated on the dock.

One boy let out a loud snort. "This sailing class is wimpy," he said. "I want to take the waterskiing class again. Nicole's a totally hot babe."

Elizabeth groaned. *It's as if someone's out there plotting against me,* she thought.

An hour into the class things had only gotten worse. In her fatigue, Elizabeth kept tripping and bumping into people as they prepared for their first outing onto the lake.

Finally Rose dismissed Elizabeth before they left the dock. "In your state you're liable to endanger the whole boat on the water," Rose said with exasperation. "You'd be better off taking a long nap."

Elizabeth bit her lip. "You're probably right, Rose. I'm sorry," she apologized. "I swear I'll get a good rest and be alert tomorrow."

"Whatever," Rose said, without meeting Elizabeth's eyes.

Feeling like a failure, Elizabeth jumped off the boat onto the dock. She had always thought of herself as a responsible person, a good role model for young kids. But now as she noticed a couple of the girls whispering and pointing at her, she knew what they were thinking. *They think I'm inept and irresponsible,* Elizabeth realized. *And they're right.*

Elizabeth trudged back to her cabin. Seeing her computer waiting for her on her bed, Elizabeth immediately forgot about resting. Her play needed just a few finishing touches. She settled down on her bunk to start writing.

One hour later Elizabeth typed THE END. Satisfied with her work, Elizabeth headed for the showers. She wanted to look fresh when she handed her play in to Joey.

"He's here!" Tanya yelled, pointing down the road at an approaching truck. Tanya had informed Jessica that just her older brother, and not her whole family, was picking her up. Since Jessica hadn't wanted Lacey to know about Tanya's hair-bleaching stunt, Jessica figured it was best to deal with the reaction to Tanya's hair by herself. After all, she could handle some sniveling teenage boy, which was how she pictured Tanya's brother.

As a muddy red pickup truck pulled into the area in front of the girls' cabins Jessica kept herself hidden in the shadows of the trees, taking the opportunity to evaluate the scene.

The car door opened and a young man stepped out. Jessica gasped. Tanya's older brother looked nothing like a sniveling teenage boy. He had black wavy hair and wore a faded plaid flannel shirt with the sleeves cut off, which showed off his muscular arms. Jessica tried not to notice how cute he was.

Tanya planted herself in front of her brother. "Hi! It's me."

His jaw dropped. "What have you *done* to yourself, you stupid little girl?"

Jessica grimaced, ducking back into the shadows.

"I dyed my hair blond," Tanya said matter-of-factly.

Tanya's brother looked around as if searching for someone to blame. "Who gave you the crazy idea to turn yourself into a dumb blonde?" he railed.

If there was one thing that made Jessica's blood boil, it was people who assumed that all blondes were dumb. She stepped out of the shadows and marched over to the truck. "Watch what you say about blondes," she said, glaring at him defiantly.

"So *you're* the one who gave Tanya the bright idea to do this," he accused.

Jessica opened her mouth to explain that she had nothing to do with it, that Tanya had done this all on her own. But when she looked at his breathtakingly perfect face, her words got caught in her throat. His eyes were so dark they were almost black, and they sparkled with a silver light. "I—she—I—" Jessica stuttered, realizing with annoyance that she was doing nothing to support her case against his "dumb blonde" comment.

Then out of the corner of her eye Jessica spotted Nicole scurrying out of the girls' cabin, clutching something to her chest. Jessica watched her for a second, her gut telling her that Nicole was up to something devious.

"What was that you were saying about 'dumb blondes'?" the guy asked sarcastically.

Jessica immediately forgot about Nicole. She turned to face the guy, who was lounging against the truck, looking arrogant. "Your little brat of a sister is the one who wants to be exactly like me," Jessica spit out. "Why don't you ask her why it's so great to be a blonde?"

Tanya burst into tears. "She called me a brat," she sobbed, running to her brother's arms.

He lifted Tanya with ease. "You have some nerve, calling my sister a brat," he said, comforting his sister. "I could report you to the camp director for that."

"So report me," Jessica dared him. They stood facing each other, their faces seething red. It was a standoff, and neither of them blinked.

"It's not even worth the trouble," the guy finally said, breaking the spell.

"Cut!" came a shout from behind them. It was Maggie. She'd caught the whole exchange on tape.

Elizabeth tucked her T-shirt into her shorts, threw her bath towel over her shoulder, and headed out of the girls' bathroom into the bright afternoon sun. She took a deep breath, filling her lungs with the fresh mountain air. Two squirrels chased each other in circles until they collided, then they disappeared up a tree. Elizabeth laughed out loud, feeling giddy. *Everything always looks a little better after a long, luxurious shower,* she thought.

Of course, the satisfaction of having finished the play contributed to Elizabeth's jubilant mood. All she had to do was pick up the computer disk and print it out in Lacey's office.

Elizabeth walked into the cabin, giving her eyes a moment to adjust to the dim light. *Where did I put the disk?* she asked herself. *Oh, right, on the table next to my bed.* She walked over to her bed and stopped. There was no disk on the table. There was a watch, a hairbrush, and a little packet of tissues, but no disk. And it wasn't on the floor next to the table. Elizabeth dropped to her knees to see if she might have accidentally kicked it under the bed. But all she saw under there were dust bunnies. The disk had disappeared. *Luckily I backed it up on the hard drive,* Elizabeth remembered with relief. She dug her laptop out of its carrying case and turned it on, searching the hard disk for *Lakeside Love*.

It was gone.

Even if someone had inadvertently taken her disk from the table, only a person with a clear motive would have gone into her computer and erased her play files.

Nicole.

Elizabeth charged out of the cabin, heading straight for main camp. She knew exactly where Nicole was—giving Joey and Maria Elizabeth's play, telling them she wrote it herself.

Nicole must have been spying on me all week, keeping tabs on my progress, Elizabeth thought with a shudder. *Then, when she saw me march happily to the showers, she sneaked in here and took it.* Approaching the drama building, Elizabeth heard Nicole's voice through the open door. "Then the stage goes black and the only thing the audience hears is the sound of chopping wood."

Elizabeth stormed up the stairs just in time to see Nicole bow and Maria and Joey break into enthusiastic applause. Elizabeth rushed into the room. "That's my play!" she yelled.

Nicole chortled. "What are you talking about? Why would I read your play?"

"Maybe because you stole it!" Elizabeth yelled, glaring at Nicole.

"Can you believe this girl?" Nicole asked Joey and Maria in fake astonishment. Then she sat down and crossed one leg over the other. "Just because I'm a quick writer with the talent it takes to knock out a fabulous play in a few short days doesn't mean there isn't room for other writers," she said. "We could use somebody to write the program copy. It's just a simple job—I'm sure you could do it."

"That's a good idea," Joey said, looking cheerfully at Elizabeth. "That way we could take advantage of your talents, too."

Maria stood up. "Yeah, Liz," she ventured. "With your skills, you'd write a program that the campers will take home with them and keep forever as a memento."

Elizabeth, who had been standing speechless, finally found her voice. "I don't want to write the program copy!" she shrieked, her fists clenched tightly. "I already wrote the play!"

Maria looked at Elizabeth and wrinkled her forehead. "But Nicole has been working on that play all week, Elizabeth," Maria said. "She's been telling me about it."

"That's because she's been sneaking onto my computer, keeping tabs on what I've written," Elizabeth cried.

Joey raised his eyebrows. "That sounds a little dubious, Liz. Nicole's a very talented writer who's had her plays produced in a number of regional theaters. Why would she steal a play from you, an untested playwright?"

"Yeah, why would I do that?" Nicole echoed, a self-satisfied grin on her face.

Joey kept his attention on Elizabeth. "Frankly, I'm a little disappointed in you," he said. "I wouldn't have expected you to be so jealous about this. We do need someone to write the program copy, but if you think that you're too good for that, we can find someone else." Joey looked at Elizabeth and shook his head.

Elizabeth felt her throat swell with frustration. *Maria and Joey believe Nicole's lie,* she realized. *I can't believe this is happening.*

"Cut!" came a shout from outside the building. Elizabeth turned to the door just in time to see Maggie scurrying away, video camera tucked under her arm.

Overwhelmed with shame, anger, and frustration, Elizabeth ran out of the building toward the thickest part of the forest surrounding the camp, tears streaming down her cheeks.

Chapter 8

"Liz! Where are you?" Maria's voice called out.

Elizabeth was sitting on a fallen tree, hugging her knees to her chest. "Here I am," she said, her voice quivering. *Maybe Maria has come to her senses,* Elizabeth hoped.

Maria appeared and sat down on the log next to Elizabeth. "Are you okay?" she asked.

Elizabeth immediately burst into tears again. "I can't believe I made such a scene back there," she sobbed.

Maria put an arm around Elizabeth's shoulders. "I must admit, I was a little shocked," she said. "It wasn't like you to act that way."

"So you know I wouldn't do that if I didn't have good reason?" Elizabeth asked, hopeful that her friend would finally see the truth.

"Well," Maria said. She bit her lip and wrung

her hands. "I know you pretty well, Elizabeth—at least I did. I know you're not the type of person to lie about something like this."

Elizabeth breathed a sigh of relief. It sounded like Maria was starting to believe her. "You don't know how happy I am to hear you say that, Maria," she said.

Then Maria shook her head. "But I think I know Nicole pretty well, too, and I just can't believe that she'd do something so devious." Maria looked up into the trees and sighed. "I don't know who to believe!"

Now Elizabeth was overcome with self-righteous anger. *Does she actually think I'm so stupid that I'd claim I'd written something I hadn't? Considering how close we were, Maria should know me better than that,* Elizabeth thought. Before she could stop herself, the floodgates of frustration opened. "I always thought of you as a perceptive person, Maria," she said bitingly. "I can't believe Nicole's got you so fooled that you don't even see what a lying, conniving creep she really is."

Maria's face fell.

Elizabeth knew immediately that she had been overly harsh. But before Elizabeth could apologize, Maria jumped up from the log and ran back through the trees. "Maria, wait!" Elizabeth called out to her. "I'm sorry! It's not *you* I'm mad at."

But Maria didn't slow down.

Elizabeth started sobbing all over again. Had

she ruined her fragile new friendship with Maria beyond repair?

"Have you ever seen a more stupid movie?" Lila leaned over and whispered to Odette.

"I don't know whose bright idea it was to make a movie about a superhero who can't even talk," Odette whispered back.

For Friday night festivities Lacey had proudly announced that the camp had gotten an advance copy of *The Adventures of the Psychic Avenger.* It was a big snore, and everyone was fidgeting in their seats.

"I haven't been this bored since my sixth-grade teacher made us sit through a twelve-part public television miniseries on farming in the foothills of Mount Everest," Odette continued.

"That sounds fascinating compared to this." Lila snorted. They both giggled. Lila had struck up a sort of friendship with Odette. Even though Odette was a nerd, at least she was a human being. The rest of Lila's campers were monsters.

Lila felt a hand on her shoulder. "Could you keep it down?" Tiffany snapped. "We're trying to pay attention."

"Yeah, you'd think a counselor wouldn't be so rude," Amber added.

"Where did you learn your manners, Lila Fowler?" Samantha said cruelly.

Lila rolled her eyes. *They don't like the movie any more than I do, and if they're paying attention, then I'm sitting here reciting Shakespeare's sonnets in my head.* Even Lacey sneaked out the back door, glancing furtively to see if anyone had noticed.

As soon as Lacey was gone Winston Egbert raced up to the front of the room, standing in the movie projector's beam of light.

"Hey, you criminal!" Winston called out in a comically gruff voice. "You stop doing that bad stuff right now or I'll call your mother."

Everyone in the audience laughed, and Winston switched to a high falsetto. "Oh, gee, Mr. Psychic Avenger, I'll stop stealing things right now. Please don't call my mother."

The laughter grew louder. Winston was a lot more entertaining than the movie. Even Lila was amused.

Then Lila felt a hand on her shoulder again. Lila groaned, expecting another snide comment from Tiffany. But when she turned around, the girl next to Tiffany was handing her a folded piece of paper.

Lila felt her heart pound in her chest as she slowly opened the note.

I'm watching you, Lila read. Down in the corner was scrawled the name *Bo.*

Lila's heart raced madly. She craned her neck, scanning the darkened room, looking for him. She spotted Bo two rows behind her, across the aisle on the boys' side. He waved. Lila waved back.

"Who are you waving at?" Amber asked, pursing her pink lips.

"None of your business," Lila snapped.

"Lila's got a boyfriend, Lila's got a boyfriend," Tiffany chanted.

Lila didn't even try to shut her up—she was too busy figuring out how she could hook up with Bo after the silly movie was over.

When Lila turned around to face forward, she saw that Winston had moved on from his impressions of the Psychic Avenger to an impression of Lacey. "This camp has been in my family since I was a little girl growing up in the back roads of Alabama before the Civil War," he said in his falsetto, mimicking Lacey's southern accent.

"Just what do you think you're doing?" Lacey's voice came from the back of the room. She stormed to the front. "Turn on the lights! Stop the film projector! Everyone back to your cabins this instant!" she barked.

Lila watched forlornly as the boys' side was hustled out first.

Just before he exited, Bo turned around and met Lila's eyes across a sea of children. He blew her a kiss.

Will I ever get to kiss him for real? Lila wondered in frustration.

That night Elizabeth was too upset to sleep. She decided to take a walk by the lake to try to figure out a way to get through the ordeal that camp had turned out to be.

As she walked through the dark forest, Elizabeth thought back with nostalgia to her happy anticipation of being a counselor. It had turned into the worst experience of her life. *Maybe if I just look at what's going on here more systematically, it won't seem so bad,* she decided.

Elizabeth cataloged her concerns one by one. First there were the terrible brats who made every day a nightmare. Then there was Nicole, the worst enemy she had ever had. Joey added a confusing element to her misery; seeing him made Elizabeth feel wonderful and horrible at the same time. The crush would have felt good, if it hadn't been compounded by her guilt about Todd.

Then there was the Maria situation. That was a total disaster. Maria seemed different—detached. She had lost the spark that used to make her so much fun to be around. *And if there had been any chance before of us re-creating our bond, I've ruined it now,* Elizabeth thought sadly. *Maria thinks I'm a malicious liar.*

As she stumbled through the dark woods Elizabeth knew she was getting farther and farther from the camp. The trees were starting to look more ominous, and the hoot of an owl made

Elizabeth jump. She was just about to turn around when she heard some giggling in the woods.

She stopped. Ten yards away Nicole and Joey sat snuggled together against a tree. Elizabeth's heart plunged.

She felt totally alone.

Then she thought of Todd. Seeing his sparkling brown eyes in her imagination, Elizabeth wondered why she was even thinking about Joey. *Why would I choose a risky, fleeting summer romance over the security of a warm, steady relationship?* Elizabeth asked herself. *Todd loves me so much, he's already sent me two postcards and a letter. And I haven't written him anything.*

Tiptoeing away, Elizabeth decided to go back to the cabin and write to Todd.

A few minutes later she was settled in her bunk, writing by the light of her flashlight.

Camp isn't quite what I imagined it would be, Elizabeth started. *Or maybe I'm not quite the counselor I imagined myself to be.*

She proceeded to write about her problematic campers, then about her disappointing reunion with Maria. Even though the problems didn't go away, writing them down always made Elizabeth feel better. And it was a relief to know Todd would understand completely.

Except that she had left out one big part of her misery: Joey. *Like I could really write to Todd about that,* Elizabeth thought. *Besides, Joey doesn't matter at this point anyway—he thinks I'm a world-class loser.* She shook her head sadly as she remembered the disappointed look on Joey's face after her outburst in the drama cabin.

Elizabeth felt her mind wander, thinking about Joey's red lips, his passionate way of speaking, his curly brown hair that she so longed to touch. She felt her fingers tingle.

Then Elizabeth looked down at the letter she was writing to her boyfriend. *Poor Todd,* she thought, feeling a wave of pity. *He doesn't deserve to be treated this way, and I don't deserve him.* Elizabeth thought back to their last conversation at Miller's Point. *Todd's jealousy sounded so strange to me then. He obviously knew something I didn't know—that I couldn't be trusted with his love.*

Elizabeth tossed the notebook on the floor and turned out the light.

"Jess! Are you awake?" Lila shook Jessica's shoulder. Jessica snuggled farther under her blanket, making sleepy noises. "Jess! I know you're awake," Lila whispered more loudly. "Don't try to pretend you don't hear me."

Jessica threw off the covers and sat up, glaring at Lila in the dark. "What is it?" she whispered, sounding annoyed.

"I'm sorry to wake you up," Lila said as sincerely

as she could. "But I can't fall asleep. I just can't let another day go by without seeing Bo."

Jessica fell back on the bed and looked up at the ceiling. "Bo, Bo, Bo," she murmured. "It's as if you've been shot by Cupid's arrow."

"I have!" Lila bubbled. "Please, I need to sneak out tonight and canoe across the lake. It's the only way we can be together."

"Who's stopping you?" Jessica grumbled, turning over to face the wall.

"Jess, I can't go alone—you've got to come with me," Lila begged, pulling on Jessica's shoulder. "I'm scared to go out on the lake by myself."

"Scared of what? Alligators?" Jessica asked sarcastically.

"That woodsman story still has me freaked out," Lila whispered, her eyes wide. "What if it's true?"

Jessica groaned. "I can't believe you fell for that. Lacey probably made up the legend to keep everyone inside at night," she said.

Lila ignored her. "I swear I'll do anything you ask for the next week," she pleaded. "Anything."

"Forget it. I'm tired," Jessica murmured.

Lila tried to assume a humble expression, but she wasn't exactly sure how to achieve it. She bit her lip. "Please, please, please, please, please," Lila groveled. "I'm begging you, Jess. I'll go out of my mind if I don't see Bo."

Jessica looked at Lila and sighed. "Even if I

don't go with you, you'll never let me get back to sleep, will you?"

Lila shook her head.

"Okay, I'll go," she said, dragging herself out of bed. "But you owe me, Lila Fowler. Big time."

"C'mon! Let's go," Lila whispered. Jessica was fussing with the canoe, pushing it farther into the brush.

"I just want to make sure it's really hidden," Jessica said, moving some branches over it.

"It's hidden, it's hidden," Lila said urgently. She grabbed Jessica's arm and tugged. "This way."

Jessica held the flashlight as the two of them crept through the woods in search of the boys' cabins.

They reached a clearing, and in the moonlight Lila could make out the outlines of a cluster of buildings. She wasn't entirely sure which building the JCs slept in, but she figured that the boys' JC cabin would be the smallest since the girls' was. Lila pointed to what looked like the smallest building. "That's the JC cabin over there, don't you think?" Lila asked Jessica.

"You mean you dragged me all the way here and you don't even know where Bo sleeps?" Jessica asked, her voice rising.

"Shhh! Keep it down," Lila whispered. "We don't want to wake up the camp. Anyway, I'm almost positive that's the one. Don't worry."

"With you in charge? I'll worry, all right," Jessica said. But she followed Lila toward the building.

Now Lila just had to decide which window was above Bo's bed. She closed her eyes and forced her mind to think of Bo's sleeping face. When she opened her eyes, they immediately fell on one of the windows. "There," Lila said, walking up under the window. "Shine the flashlight in here," she told Jessica. "I can feel that Bo is on the other side."

One second later the unmistakable face of Winston Egbert popped into the flashlight's beam. "Who's there?" he called.

Jessica gasped. "Winston!" She dropped her flashlight and the light went out.

"Jessica!" Lila scolded. "Now I can't see a thing!"

"I didn't do it on purpose," Jessica hissed.

"Be quiet and find it," Lila hissed back. The girls stumbled around in the darkness while Lila prayed that Winston wouldn't bust them.

Suddenly there was a huge crash and Jessica yelped. "I stubbed my toe into a trash can," she whined.

Lila threw up her hands in despair. "You're the clumsiest, most unre—"

A male voice interrupted Lila. "Who's out here?"

"Here's the flashlight!" Jessica whispered. She turned on the flashlight and directed it at the cabin.

Lila gasped. Five guys stood in the doorway, dressed in their pajamas.

"You girls look lost," one of the guys said with a

131

laugh. Lila recognized Bo's voice instantly. "Why don't you come in out of the cold?"

"We thought you'd never ask," Lila said. She marched inside and Jessica followed.

"So what brought you to our side of camp?" Justin asked the girls after they sat down on one of the beds.

"Well, we were on our way into town when we dropped our compass into the lake, so we had no choice but to come to the boys' camp," Jessica joked flirtatiously.

Lila smiled. *The old Wakefield charm is coming back,* she thought.

Bo sat down on the bed next to Lila. "It's really cool to see you, Lila. Sorry I'm so sleepy," he said, running his fingers through his unruly hair.

Lila wished they were alone so that she could be the one caressing his hair. "That's okay," she said, taking his hand. "I'm just happy to be talking to you—finally. I haven't stopped thinking about you since we talked at breakfast on Tuesday," she admitted shyly.

"Really?" Bo asked.

Lila nodded. "Really."

Then Jessica leaned across Lila's lap. "If you don't believe her, you can ask me," she said. "I haven't stopped hearing about you."

"Jess," Lila said, giving Jessica a playful shove. Lila was in heaven. She and Bo weren't alone, but

132

it still felt good to be with him. It also didn't hurt that there were four other young guys drooling over the girls.

"What's that noise?" Jessica asked suddenly.

Everyone stopped talking to listen. It was unmistakable—someone was chopping wood right outside the cabin!

Lila started screaming hysterically. "It's the woodsman! It's the woodsman!"

Aaron and Justin jumped up and ran to the door. Jessica followed. Bo dove under his covers.

Lila heard Derek's voice outside. "That's enough, Buford. You can quit chopping wood."

Everyone in the cabin groaned.

Then Buford rushed in. "Did I scare you guys?" he asked excitedly.

Bo threw off his covers. "Oh, please. Like we really thought a ghost was out there," he said, looking right past Lila.

He can't even look at me, he thinks I'm such a dope, Lila realized. Stifling a sob, she ran out of the cabin.

Jessica ran to catch up with her. "Lila! What happened? Why'd you run off so suddenly?"

"Oh, Jess, I've ruined my chances with Bo," she wailed, falling into Jessica outstretched arms. "Bo thinks I'm a hysterical wimp."

"Why, because you got scared in there?" Jessica asked. "Bo was the one who dove under his covers," she said with a shrug.

Lila rubbed the back of her hand across her tear-streaked face. "That's just it," she sobbed. "He was making fun of how scared I was. Bo is one of the bravest guys I've ever met. He would never have gotten spooked by Buford's silly prank."

Jessica wrinkled her forehead. "Are you sure about that?"

"Do you know how many times Bo has risked his life just for the fun of it?" Lila asked.

"I have a feeling I'm soon going to learn." Jessica sighed. "C'mon, Li. Let's go get the canoe." She hooked her arm through Lila's and led her down to the canoe's hiding place.

Rowing over the still water, Lila cursed herself for botching all the progress she'd made with Bo. Then she stopped. *What am I getting all upset about?* she asked herself. *The only way to win is never to give up. I'll just have to figure out a way to prove to Bo that I'm a strong, self-sufficient, nature-loving woman.*

Then she had a brainstorm. "Jess?" she called up to the front of the canoe. "When you went on your Death Valley adventure, did you learn how to make a fire using sticks?"

"Yeah, why?" Jessica called back.

Lila smiled. *That should do the trick,* she said to herself.

Chapter 9

"Diz! Watch where you heap those potatoes," Nicole scolded. "You're getting mashed potatoes in the corn compartment."

Elizabeth gritted her teeth. "Sorry." Elizabeth and Nicole had been assigned food-serving duties that night. The hatred between them was electric.

Nicole sighed loudly. "Did you see the new camp T-shirt that Joey was wearing last night?"

"I didn't notice," Elizabeth answered flatly.

"Oh, right—of course you wouldn't have seen it," Nicole said with a secretive smile. "He didn't put it on until late, after almost everyone was in bed."

If this isn't cruel and unusual punishment, I don't know what is, Elizabeth said to herself as she spooned mashed potatoes onto the passing trays.

"Oh, I meant to tell you—thanks for the play," Nicole said suddenly.

Elizabeth turned to look at Nicole's odious face, nearly choking on her anger. She had already known that Nicole stole her play, but the way she so brazenly admitted her thievery filled Elizabeth with even more rage. "I'll get even with you, you lying snake," Elizabeth swore.

Nicole laughed. "I'm shaking in my shoes."

Elizabeth swallowed her anger, methodically scooping potatoes onto the trays in front of her. "Do you want lots of mashed potatoes or just a little?" she asked the young boy standing with his tray held out.

The boy looked at the light gray lumps of potatoes piled onto Elizabeth's spoon, then looked up at Elizabeth. "I don't know. Did you make it?"

"No," Elizabeth answered.

"It sure looks like your face," the boy joked, doubling over in laughter.

The boy next in line joined in. "Yeah!" he cried. "Ug-ly!"

"That's not very nice," Elizabeth said weakly.

The boys laughed even louder.

Nicole joined the boys' laughter. "Not nice, but funny," she said with a giggle. "Have some corn, you little comedians," she said. The boys held out their trays and looked up at Nicole in awe as she dropped perfect little piles of corn kernels right into the appropriate compartment on their trays.

"I don't see you laughing, Elizabeth," Nicole

said. "Don't you have a sense of humor?"

Elizabeth grimaced. "With you standing next to me, no, I don't."

"Oooh, that's not very nice," Nicole mimicked Elizabeth's earlier statement in a childish voice.

"Let's just do our jobs and get this over with," Elizabeth grumbled.

Nicole shrugged. "Suit yourself."

Finally the line of campers had all been fed. Elizabeth and Nicole filled their trays with food and headed for the tables.

Elizabeth stood holding her tray, looking for Jessica and Lila. Suddenly someone bumped her from behind, and her cup of bug juice splashed all down her front. Elizabeth groaned.

Nicole brushed by her. "So sorry," she apologized insincerely.

Without thinking, Elizabeth dumped macaroni and cheese on Nicole's rear end. "Whoops," she said.

Nicole turned around and glared at Elizabeth.

Elizabeth smiled. "How about some corn to go with your mac and cheese?" she asked, tossing handfuls of corn down Nicole's V-neck shirt collar.

"You little wench!" Nicole spit back, pouring her peas over Elizabeth's head.

"Food fight!" someone yelled from a nearby table. One minute later there was food flying everywhere, with Elizabeth and Nicole in the thick of it.

Half of the campers ducked under the tables

137

while the other half raced around the room, lobbing handfuls of corn, peas, mashed potatoes, and macaroni into the air, onto the walls, and straight at each other. Counselors and JCs rushed around frantically, trying to regain control.

Meanwhile Maggie scurried through the brawl, dodging the flying food, ducking between the fighting parties, her camera whirring. She stopped only when someone threw mashed potatoes at her lens.

Suddenly an earsplitting shriek filled the room. Elizabeth stopped midthrow to cover her ears. She looked up to see Joey standing on a chair in the middle of the room. He held a silver whistle in his hand, and Lacey stood stern-faced beside him.

"You two!" Lacey barked, looking straight at Elizabeth and Nicole. "In my office! Now!"

Elizabeth turned crimson as she and Nicole followed Lacey's stiff figure out of the mess hall.

Inside Lacey's office Elizabeth waited for Lacey to speak first. But Nicole didn't.

"It all started when Elizabeth threw macaroni and cheese on me for no reason!" Nicole cried.

Lacey raised her eyebrows. "Did you throw macaroni and cheese on Nicole?" she asked Elizabeth.

"Only after she spilled bug juice down my front," Elizabeth said defensively.

"I did not spill bug juice down your front. You

spilled bug juice down your front," Nicole shouted back.

"After you bumped into me!"

"Have you ever heard of an accident? I said I was sorry!"

"You said it but you didn't mean it," Elizabeth spit out.

"Girls! Stop your screeching!" Lacey commanded.

Elizabeth looked down in shame. She'd never heard herself sound so immature before in her life.

Lacey turned to Nicole. "Nicole, you say you bumped into Elizabeth and she spilled her drink?"

"Yes, Lacey, and I said I was sorry. Then before I knew it, I had macaroni and cheese all over my behind," Nicole said, standing up and turning so Lacey could see the yellow mess on her white shorts.

Lacey clucked. She turned her gaze to Elizabeth. "It sounds like you created quite a scene, young lady. I've never seen such childish, irresponsible behavior coming from one of my junior counselors," she said. "And this isn't the first complaint we've had about you. Rose tells me that you haven't been much of an assistant to her. She even had to dismiss you from workshop yesterday." Lacey paused and shook her head. "I'd just like to know why you can't act more like your sister, Jessica—hardworking, sensible, honest. I thought

139

identical twins were supposed to be more alike."

Elizabeth couldn't believe her ears. *Is this a nightmare?* she wondered in horror.

Where's Jess when I need her? I'm having a crisis here! Lila wailed silently. She had already gone through four outfits, but not one of them had the appropriate mix of wholesomeness and alluring sophistication she was trying to achieve. She collapsed on her bed, feeling her usual cool manner dissipate as an anxiety attack threatened to burst forth.

Just then Jessica bounded into the cabin. "Lacey's given me the keys to her Bronco to drive into town for provisions for the dance tomorrow," Jessica said cheerfully. "Do you want to come with me?"

"Oh, Jess! Thank goodness you're here," Lila gushed. "I'm having an outfit emergency."

"You're having an outfit emergency about taking a ride into town?" Jessica asked with a laugh.

"Taking a ride into town? I'm not going into town," Lila said, confused.

"But I just asked—"

"Jess!" Lila stood up from her bed. "Could you just shut up for one minute and help me figure out what I should wear for my date with Bo?"

"You have a date with Bo tonight?" Jessica asked, sitting down on her bunk. "When did he ask you out? I thought you hadn't seen him since you humiliated yourself last night."

"Thanks for reminding me, Jess," Lila moaned. "I could use a little support here."

Jessica sat on Lila's bunk. "I'm sorry, Li. I'm just surprised that you have a date with him."

Lila sat down next to her. "Well, we don't really have a date in the literal sense of the word. I just know deep down that there's nothing he'd rather do on his free Saturday night than be with me. But this is all irrelevant anyway," she said with a dismissive wave of her hand. "What matters here is that tonight's the night I have to prove to him that I'm a nature-loving, adventurous type of girl or our romance is doomed before it ever got a chance to blossom."

"And there's no one more nature-loving or adventurous than you, Lila Fowler," Jessica said with a smirk.

"Cut the sarcasm, Wakefield, and give me some advice here," Lila replied.

"OK, OK, calm down," Jessica soothed. "Your own personal fashion adviser is here to save the day."

Together they found an ideal outfit: khaki designer slacks that fit perfectly and would protect Lila's legs against hungry bugs and a royal blue cotton knit sweater vest worn over a white T-shirt.

Lila stood on a chair to survey the complete look in the small mirror on the wall. She jumped down, satisfied that she looked both casual and sexy. "Thanks, Jess! You're the greatest," she said, hugging her friend. She started walking out of the cabin, then stopped and turned around. "What are you doing tonight, anyway?"

Jessica sighed. "Going into town to get provisions for the dance tomorrow night, remember?"

"Right, have fun!" Lila called over her shoulder as she set off to find Bo.

But after looking in the most likely places, Lila was stumped. Bo wasn't in the main lodge, he wasn't by the lake, he wasn't in the counselors' rec room. Then Lila saw Buford and Johansen coming toward the center of camp from the direction of the boys' cabins, so she asked them if they'd seen Bo.

"He left the cabin over an hour ago," Buford told her. "He didn't say what he was doing."

"We're trying to round up some people for a game of Hearts," Johansen said. "If you find Bo, the two of you should come down to the rec room. It'll be real fun."

"Yeah, you should come," Buford agreed.

Lila bit back the urge to laugh. *Lila Fowler, playing a boring old card game on a Saturday night? I don't think so,* she joked to herself. "Thanks, but we have other plans," Lila said, enjoying their pitifully disappointed expressions as they shuffled away.

She returned to her search for Bo. *Where could*

he be on a Saturday night? Lila wondered. *Is he with another girl?* Lila pushed that pessimistic thought right out of her mind. *Of course he isn't with another girl. Who could compete with Lila Fowler?*

Lila circled back around all the main cabins, thinking she might have missed him down by the lake since it was so dark. Bo had told her how much he liked his solitude and how much he liked being out in the wilderness. *I bet he's converging with nature, spearing fish, or trapping wild animals or something,* Lila figured.

She was walking by one of the workshop cabins and was surprised to see a light on inside. That was odd—workshops were over for the evening.

Lila peeked in a window and saw dozens of hanging plants and terrariums. It was the nature cabin. And there was Bo, all alone, humming to himself as he watered plants and checked on seedlings.

"You're growing big and tall," Bo murmured to a small plant as he fingered it lovingly.

This didn't compute. Bo—Mr. Rough and Tough—talking to plants?

Lila stood in the doorway and cleared her throat.

Bo turned, startled. "Hey, Lila," he said shyly.

"Hi, Bo," Lila said. "What are you doing here all by yourself?"

143

"I'm, uh—well, see—" he stuttered, flustered. "Lacey caught me in the lounge, sitting around reading my *Mountain Adventures* magazine, and she ordered me to water these plants tonight," he mumbled. He threw back his shoulders. "It really stinks that I got stuck here with the wimps in the nature cabin," he pronounced. Then he looked at Lila. "Listen to me, complaining about being in the nature cabin. I bet you've been dying over in arts and crafts."

Lila shrugged. "Oh, it's a drag, but I'm practicing my map-making skills," she said. She wasn't about to mention that she had *requested* arts and crafts.

Bo tossed the watering can he was holding into a cabinet. "I wanted to be the riflery JC, but they never give you what you request," he said.

Lila smiled. *This is more like the Bo I know,* she thought. "When can you get out of here?" she asked him.

"Whenever. Now," Bo answered quickly.

"I'm all right, Jess. I just don't feel like going anywhere tonight," Elizabeth said. After her humiliation at dinner, Elizabeth had wandered alone through the woods. Now she sat on her bunk, watching Jessica get ready to drive into town.

"Are you sure you don't want to come with me?" Jessica asked. "I could use your help in planning the party. You're great at things like that."

Elizabeth looked at her sister and frowned. "Don't be silly. You're the one who's good at parties," she said. "Besides, considering how Lacey feels about me, I don't think she'd be too pleased if she found out I'd ridden in her car."

Jessica tossed her purse on her bed and came and sat down next to Elizabeth. "I wish you wouldn't be so hard on yourself," she said soothingly.

"Why not? I deserve it," Elizabeth moped. She lay on her back and stared at the plywood beams of the ceiling. "I think I just need to be alone."

Jessica sat still for a moment, watching Elizabeth. "I hate to leave you alone like this," she said. "I wish there were something I could do to lift you out of your doldrums."

Elizabeth turned her head to look at her sister. "I already told you what you could do. You could leave me alone." Her voice came out harsher than she had intended.

Jessica looked hurt. "Fine," she said. She snatched her purse from her bed and strode out of the cabin.

After Jessica had left, Elizabeth wished she could take back her words. She stared up at the ugly knot in the plywood ceiling above her head. It looked as ugly as Elizabeth felt. *Lacey was right*, Elizabeth thought. *I'm childish and irresponsible. I should be acting more like my sister. Jessica is the responsible one, the one Lacey feels she can trust with the keys to her car.*

Elizabeth couldn't believe how much their roles had reversed in the matter of a few short days. Was it the mountain air? The altitude? A misalignment of the planets? Whatever it was, Elizabeth now felt like a complete failure. After only one week of camp, she'd been singled out as a troublemaker.

But I'm not the only troublemaker, Elizabeth thought after a minute. *Nicole deserves most of the blame for the food fight—she started it.*

Nicole.

Elizabeth shivered with hatred just thinking her enemy's name. Nicole Banes, the bane of her existence.

Elizabeth looked over to Nicole's bunk. Without even thinking about it, she got up and started to poke around Nicole's things. *I've got to find something here that proves Nicole stole my play,* Elizabeth thought.

Then Elizabeth heard a familiar laugh from the doorway. "I know exactly what you're up to," Nicole said.

Elizabeth jumped up, flustered.

Nicole continued, "But you're not going to find what you're looking for."

Elizabeth gathered her composure. "You're a liar and a thief, Nicole Banes. You know it, and I know it," she said cuttingly. "Now I'll just have to prove to everyone else what we both know is true—that you stole the play I wrote and lied about writing it yourself."

Nicole laughed again. "You'll never be able to prove that I stole your play, so you might as well give up trying," she said airily. She pushed Elizabeth aside and reached into her makeup case, pulling out an emery board. "There's absolutely no evidence. I covered all my tracks," Nicole said as she casually filed her nails.

"I bet you never wrote anything in your life," Elizabeth charged. "All those plays you were supposed to have written . . . who'd you steal those from?"

Nicole stopped filing and glared at Elizabeth.

Elizabeth glared back. Neither girl blinked. The room was silent and heavy with hatred.

Suddenly there was a crash from outside. It sounded like someone had fallen in the bushes next to the cabin.

Nicole ran to the doorway. "Who's out there?" she called. There was no response. Nicole continued out of the cabin. "I'd better see what's going on," she said over her shoulder.

"You can walk away from me, Nicole Banes, but I'll get you in the end," Elizabeth swore.

Nicole stopped and turned, placing a hand on her chest. "Is that a threat?"

"It's not a threat," Elizabeth answered. "It's a promise."

Chapter 10

Lila walked Bo to a clearing that she had scouted out that afternoon. In the daylight it had looked a little forlorn. But under the cloak of night it was perfect.

"This is beautiful," Bo said, sitting back against a boulder.

Lila sat down next to him. "Isn't it wonderful? I've come out here almost every night after everyone else is asleep," Lila lied. "I need to feel alone with nature, you know?"

Bo nodded enthusiastically. "Sure do!" he said, looking up at the sky. The night was black, and thousands of stars glistened above.

Suddenly an owl hooted and Bo jerked. "What was that?" he asked, his voice urgent. His eyes darted around the dark clearing.

"Just an owl, I think," Lila guessed.

"Right, an owl," Bo said casually. "Montana owls sound a lot different. That's why I didn't know what that was," he explained.

"Owls sound different here?" Lila asked.

"Totally different," Bo answered authoritatively.

"In what way?" Lila asked.

"Just different," Bo muttered quickly.

"Oh," Lila said. She had always thought an owl hoot was an owl hoot, but who was she to question someone as knowledgeable as Bo?

Bo grabbed for her hand. "Can we talk about something else?" He looked deep into her eyes. "Like how beautiful your eyes look in the moonlight?"

Lila smiled. "Sure, let's talk about that," she cooed, squeezing his hand. "How beautiful do my eyes look in the moonlight?"

"Very beautiful," Bo murmured.

They sat for a moment staring at each other in silence, listening to the chirp of the crickets. Somewhere in the forest a twig cracked. "What was that?" Bo exclaimed, dropping Lila's hand.

Lila rubbed her hand where it had hit a sharp pebble. "A deer or something."

"Right, a deer," Bo said. He crossed and uncrossed his legs. "So what do you want to do?" he asked.

Lila frowned. *Why is Bo so fidgety?* she wondered. *Is he getting bored with me already?* She bit her lip. *I've come this far, I'm not going to give*

150

up now, she decided. "I've got a tree-bark tea recipe for you to try," Lila said out loud. She had found the recipe in one of her nature magazines.

"Cool," Bo said, swallowing the word. "What kind of recipe?"

"Tree-bark tea," Lila repeated.

Bo still looked puzzled.

"You know, tea made from the bark of a tree?"

Bo slapped his thigh. "Right! I drink that all the time!"

Lila smiled with relief. "I just have to build a fire," she said.

"Do you have matches?" Bo asked. "Because I didn't bring any."

"Not a problem," Lila said confidently. "There are plenty of sticks and leaves around here to build a fire with."

Bo looked at Lila in astonishment. "You know how to make a fire with sticks?"

"Sure, it's no big deal," Lila said casually. Actually it was quite a big deal. Lila had been rubbing sticks together all day and her palms were dotted with blisters.

"That's really cool, Lila," Bo said appreciatively after Lila had built a small fire.

Lila shrugged. "It's a skill that comes in handy. I hate to bring matches into the wilderness. Sulfur wreaks havoc on plant life," she explained, remembering an article she had read.

Bo nodded. "True, very true."

Lila took a sip of the tea she'd made and tried not to gag. "I like to live off the land whenever possible," she boasted proudly.

"Me too," Bo agreed. He polished off his first cup of tea, then poured himself another.

Lila forced herself to drink more, too.

Then Bo put down his cup and looked at Lila intently. "I've never gone out with someone like you," he said. "Most of the girls I've gone out with are so—" He stopped.

"So what?" Lila prodded him.

"I don't know . . . fragile, I guess. The way you're so strong and brave makes me feel like—" He paused again. "I just hope I'm strong enough for you," he said finally.

"I'm sure you'll do fine," Lila said with a smile. She reached out and squeezed his right bicep. It felt as hard as the boulder they were leaning on. "Wow! I guess this is from all the rock climbing you do," Lila said admiringly. "I've been meaning to ask you if you'll give me a lesson—after skydiving, it's the one thing I've always wanted to try."

"Yeah, I guess I could," Bo said, rubbing his arm shyly.

He looked so cute and modest, Lila impulsively threw her arms around him. Their lips met in a passionate kiss.

Bo pulled back from their embrace and looked

Lila solemnly in the eyes. "Lila, have I remembered to tell you that you're the most beautiful girl I've ever met?" Bo asked, his voice husky.

"I think you forgot," Lila said.

"Well, you are," he replied.

They kissed. It was deep and slow. Lila felt faint. She had debated with herself about whether to bring up the incident in the boys' cabin the night before, but the way the night was going, she knew it was a nonissue. Why bring up the painful past?

Then Lila heard the nighttime bugle call signaling lights out in fifteen minutes.

"I guess we'd better get back to camp," Bo said, touching Lila's cheek.

"I guess so," she said sadly, staring straight into his beautiful eyes. Lila took Bo's hand and squeezed it. "So, Bo," she said flirtatiously. "Should I sleep in my clothes tonight just in case someone comes knocking on my window?" She batted her eyes, waiting for his enthusiastic response to her invitation.

He looked at her, then looked down at the ground in front of him. "Gee, Lila . . ." he started hesitantly.

Lila sucked in her breath, waiting for his next words. She wouldn't be able to bear it if he rejected her.

Bo continued, "You know, I'm not sure that's such a good idea—"

Lila yanked her hand out of his grasp. "Sure, fine, forget it," she said quickly.

"It's just that there was trouble last time you snuck over, and—"

"Don't even bother trying to explain!" Lila interrupted him. She didn't want to hear his lame excuses. She had to keep some dignity. She jumped up and ran out of the clearing before he could see the tears that threatened to trickle from her eyes.

"Lila, wait!" Bo called after her.

But Lila didn't stop. She ran all the way back to the girls' cabins, tears of frustration streaming down her face.

All my work was for nothing, she realized. *Bo can see I'm a fraud.*

At Sunday brunch Jessica's girls watched as she mixed up her home fries and scrambled eggs. After a moment they mixed theirs up, too.

"I like to mix my potatoes with my eggs," Anastasia announced to the table with a shake of her black curls.

"Me too," echoed Sofia, her big brown eyes staring at Jessica with admiration.

"Me thwee," Stephanie chirped, bouncing up and down.

"I got black stuff in mine!" Sarah wailed.

Anastasia reached over and pulled a long strand

of Sarah's hair off her plate. "That's your hair, silly."

Maggie videotaped the whole exchange.

Jessica just ate her breakfast. By this time she had figured out that the best way to deal with the Wannabees' constant mimicry was to try not to think about it too much. Besides, when it wasn't annoying, it was cute.

Jessica turned around to the next table, where Lila and the Sulky Six were sitting. "So how did your date go last night?" she whispered to Lila.

"I don't want to talk about it," Lila whispered back.

Jessica raised her eyebrows. "Why not? What happened?"

"I don't want to talk about it," Lila snapped, her voice loud and coarse.

"Our fearless leader seems to be in a snit this morning," Samantha said saucily. "Get out of the wrong side of bed?"

Nancy flipped her shoulder-length brown hair over one shoulder. "I think I saw her with that cute nature guy last night," she said, her voice dripping with insinuation. "They looked chummy when I saw them."

"Did he come to his senses later and realize what an airhead you are?" Robin asked Lila, her green eyes flashing.

"Or did he get too fresh with you?" Tiffany taunted.

Lila glared at Jessica.

Jessica frowned in apology. She hadn't meant for Lila's girls to terrorize her—she just wanted to know why Lila was so glum that morning. Jessica turned back to her breakfast and picked up a sausage. She nibbled on it, ignoring the way Sofia, Anastasia, Maggie, Stephanie, and Sarah nibbled on their sausages, too. Jessica glanced over to where Elizabeth sat with her group, a few tables away.

"Jennifer! Stop pouring milk in your eggs," Jessica heard Elizabeth bark.

"But I like them that way," Jennifer sniveled.

"Fine, whatever," Elizabeth grumbled. As the rest of her girls started pouring milk into their eggs, Elizabeth put her face in her hands, looking completely forlorn.

Jessica's heart went out to her sister. She knew how humiliated Elizabeth was about her public flogging by Lacey the night before. And Jessica couldn't help but notice that a number of the campers were pointing at her twin, laughing and making jokes about her. *Poor Liz. She doesn't deserve this*, Jessica thought.

It's so strange that both Lila and Elizabeth are miserable and I'm having a great time, Jessica thought. *It's got to be because of my no-guy rule*, she decided.

Then Tanya appeared in front of Jessica. "Hi, Jess, I'm back," Tanya announced, squeezing herself between Jessica and Stephanie.

"I see your hair has gone back to normal,"

156

Jessica said, taking in Tanya's natural-looking hair.

"Yeah, my mom fixed it," Tanya said casually.

Jessica brushed her fingers through Tanya's hair. "Well, she did a good job," Jessica said. "I think you look better as a speckled blond, anyway."

"My brother Paul kept asking about you all weekend," Tanya announced loudly.

Jessica felt her stomach lurch. She had done her best to forget about Tanya's brother, but now she knew his name. Paul.

Tanya continued merrily. "He wouldn't stop talking about you—Jessica this, Jessica that, who is that Jessica girl?"

Lila leaned over from her table. "*Paul?*" she asked, raising her eyebrows. "Why didn't you tell me about *Paul?*"

"There's nothing to tell," Jessica hissed. "He's just Tanya's older brother. I met him when he picked her up on Friday."

"Girls think my brother's a dreamboat," Tanya said with pride. "I hear them talking about him when they come by the restaurant. They say, 'I wish they'd put Paul on the menu. I'd order him in a minute,'" she mimicked.

"He was a jerk," Jessica said quietly to Lila so that Tanya wouldn't hear. "Even if I were in the market for a guy—which I'm not—Paul is probably the last person I'd be interested in."

Lila just smiled.

* * *

"Need some help with that?" Jessica heard someone say from the doorway behind her. It was Derek, the tumbling instructor.

Jessica jumped down from a chair. "Oh, thanks, Derek. I can't seem to reach quite high enough to hang these lights from the ceiling beam." Jessica was spending her free Sunday afternoon in the main lodge, stringing little white lights all around the room in preparation for the dance that night.

"I can get that for you. Move aside," Derek said valiantly, taking the mass of wires and light-bulbs from Jessica's arms. He climbed up on the chair, effortlessly reaching the beam with his long, muscular arms, and wrapped some of the lights around it. Then he jumped down and moved the chair a few feet, climbed up, and wrapped some more. He continued around the room as Jessica moved on to the task of gluing together small replicas of the camp flag.

"What else can I do?" Derek asked when he had finished with the lights.

Jessica shrugged. "You could help me with these flags," she replied.

"Be glad to," Derek said enthusiastically. He settled down at the table across from her and went diligently to work.

Jessica looked across the table at Derek's handsome face. If she had doubted it before, now

158

Jessica knew that Derek had a thing for her. But even though he was really cute and nice, Jessica didn't feel any sparks. *At least, not the kind of sparks that flew when I met Paul,* Jessica thought.

Jessica's mind wandered to Tanya's news flash this morning. *So Paul's been asking about me,* she mused. Since their fiery encounter two days before, Paul had been on Jessica's mind, too, even though she'd tried not to think about him. Now that she knew he'd been thinking about her, she allowed herself to remember how sexy he was.

Jessica felt a tremble as the delicious feeling of wanting someone washed over her. For the first time in weeks she felt close to her normal self. *I need that feeling,* she realized.

Jessica thought back to the last guy who had made her feel this way. *Christian.* Jessica put the bottle of glue down on the table as memories of Christian washed over her. His laugh, his dark brown hair, his powerful surfer's body. *What might we have become together if Christian hadn't been stolen away from me so quickly?* Jessica wondered. Then she forced herself not to think about it. She had to move on.

Maybe Lila is right, Jessica thought. *Maybe another guy is exactly what I need to get over the heartbreak I suffered after Christian.* Even though acting responsible and dependable had its moments, it wasn't the true Jessica. Neither was the no-guy rule. The true Jessica loved guys, *thrived* on guys!

There was no doubt about it: Jessica had to see Paul again, no matter what. With a quickly beating heart, she started planning a field trip for herself. She still had the keys to Lacey's Bronco—she could sneak back into town late that night and find the restaurant Tanya's parents owned. Jessica's hands shook with excitement at the thought of seeing Paul.

Then she gave herself a paper cut. "Ouch," she cried, lifting her finger to her mouth.

"Are you okay?" Derek asked.

Jessica looked up, startled. She had totally forgotten Derek was even in the room. The sight of his needy, adoring face repelled Jessica. It painfully reminded her too much of Ken.

Ken. Jessica had loved Ken for quite a while. He'd been a sweetheart and a true friend right up until the end. But her love for him hadn't been able to match the power of the emotions she'd felt for Christian.

And here was Derek—who could have been Ken's identical cousin—looking completely lovestruck. The butterflies in Jessica's stomach turned to nausea. She felt sick.

Derek's face darkened with concern. "You don't look like you feel very well. Can I get you something?" he asked, taking Jessica's hand.

Jessica gently pulled her hand away. "No, that's okay," she said. *The only thing that would make me feel better is to see Paul again,* Jessica added silently. *How can I stand not seeing him until tonight?* Then Jessica remembered that Maggie had videotaped her first meeting with Paul when he had come to pick up Tanya. *If I can't see him this afternoon, at least I can let my eyes feast on his gorgeous videotaped self.*

Jessica jumped up from the table to find Maggie. She needed the tape!

"Where are you going?" Derek asked as Jessica dashed out of the lodge.

"I have to pick up some stuff!" Jessica shouted. "Don't bother with the rest. I'll get to it later."

Jessica left a surprised Derek and ran all the way to the girls' cabins. Maggie's room was empty, but her video camera was lying on her bunk. So Jessica took the liberty of taking the tape out of the camera. Then she ran all the way back into the counselors' rec room, where she knew there was a VCR.

She scanned the tape and quickly found the section with Paul. Jessica's heart swelled on seeing his face again. She rewound his section over and over again, relishing the emotion it awakened in her. She barely breathed as she drank in his rugged beauty.

Finally Jessica felt satisfied. She let the rest of the tape run.

161

The tape was actually pretty funny. Maggie had a knack for catching people at awkward, revealing moments. There was Elizabeth mumbling to herself at the campfire. There was Lacey, tripping up the steps of her office. There was Winston, doing a belly flop into the lake. It was kind of like watching one of those home-video blooper shows.

All of a sudden Nicole and Elizabeth came on the screen.

Jessica's jaw dropped as she watched the scene unfold. "This is incredible!" she said to the empty room.

Jessica snatched the tape from the machine and raced out of the office.

Elizabeth lay on her bed, staring up at the same ugly knot in the plywood ceiling that had symbolized her despair the night before. If anything, Elizabeth's mood had deteriorated since.

If Nicole had shown even the tiniest bit of remorse or shame about her devious betrayal, Elizabeth might have felt a little better. But Nicole didn't seem to be suffering in the least. The fact that Elizabeth was the one who'd been wronged and the only one who was suffering made her feel like a total failure as a person.

Suddenly Elizabeth heard Jessica's voice over the PA system.

"Will all campers, JCs, and counselors please

come to the main lodge for a special presentation," Jessica's voice echoed through the camp. "One of my campers has a big surprise."

What could Jessica be up to? Elizabeth wondered. *Should I even bother going to find out?* She wasn't really in the mood to face everyone and their scorn, but since she had already sunk so low in their eyes, one more appearance wouldn't make her sink any lower. And she didn't want to lie here staring at the ceiling for the rest of the afternoon— or for the rest of her life.

So curious, if unenthusiastic, she put on a fresh T-shirt and headed to the lodge.

Everyone was buzzing when Elizabeth got there.

"What's this about?" Justin asked Winston, who shrugged.

"What's she doing?" Robin asked Nancy.

"Who knows?" Nancy replied.

"I was having a perfectly good nap," Joey said grumpily. "This better be good."

Lacey walked up to Joey. "Sleeping? In the middle of the day?" She arched an eyebrow.

Joey shrugged sheepishly, and Elizabeth smiled.

Then Maria grabbed Elizabeth by the elbow. "Do you know what's up with your sister?" Maria asked.

"No, I don't," Elizabeth answered brusquely. She felt so awkward around Maria, she found it hard to be civil.

Maria shrugged and walked away, catching up with Nicole, who looked over her shoulder at Elizabeth and smirked.

Lonely and dejected, Elizabeth went into the main room and found a seat. People streamed in, but no one sat next to her. Elizabeth was starting to feel like she shouldn't have come when Lila came over and sat down. Elizabeth had never expected to see the day when she was actually grateful for Lila's company.

"What's Jess up to now?" Lila asked.

"I have no idea," Elizabeth replied.

Jessica flitted about the room, urging people to sit down. Spotting Elizabeth in her seat, Jessica smiled and waved. "You're going to love this!" she mouthed.

Finally everyone had settled in their seats.

Jessica walked to the front of the room and cleared her throat. "Some of you might be aware that one of my campers, Maggie, has been video-taping our first week here at Camp Echo Mountain," she said. Everyone broke out in titters, and Jessica smiled, looking totally in her element in front of an audience.

Jessica continued, "I've viewed the tape and decided that everyone here will get a kick out of seeing it, especially since tonight is the first big social event of camp. So without further ado, please dim the lights!"

The lights went down and the huge screen lit up with images of the past week. Various scenes moved across the screen: people being thrown in the lake, one girl getting ambushed by a mob of boys with s'mores, Bo kissing Lila's cheek, the food fight.

Elizabeth covered her eyes when she was confronted with the image of herself hurling potatoes at Nicole. When she peeked again, she gasped. There on-screen was the image of Elizabeth in the female junior counselors' cabin, rummaging around Nicole's bunk. *When was this taped?* Elizabeth wondered.

Then she heard Nicole's voice from off-screen. "I know exactly what you're up to."

The on-screen Elizabeth straightened up. "You're a liar and a thief, Nicole Banes. You know it, and I know it," she said, glaring at the still off-screen Nicole.

Elizabeth gasped. *This is the fight I had with Nicole last night in the cabin!* she realized in shock. So someone had been out there causing that commotion: Maggie, with her video camera. Elizabeth watched the scene unfold with rapt attention. She noticed that even in the dim light of the cabin, the camera still picked up the haughty expression on Nicole's face as she swaggered into the frame.

"You'll never be able to prove that I stole your play, so you might as well give up trying," Nicole's videotaped image said. "There's absolutely no evidence. I covered all my tracks." Nicole casually began filing her nails as if she didn't have a care in the world.

Elizabeth heard a number of gasps from the audience and couldn't help smiling broadly.

Suddenly the frame jumped and bobbed, indicating when Maggie must have lost her footing.

The lights went up to reveal Nicole, crouched over, trying to sneak out the back exit.

"Ms. Banes!" Lacey bellowed. "I hope you're on your way to my office, because we have some serious matters to discuss!"

Elizabeth felt her heart swell with joy. Score one round for Elizabeth Wakefield!

Chapter 11

I know I promised that I'd write you every other day, but when you hear about the week I've just had, you'll understand why I haven't had the strength to write.

Elizabeth was sitting by the lake, writing Todd a long-overdue letter. She needed some peace. After the video presentation everyone had rushed over to Elizabeth, apologizing and voicing their support. Elizabeth felt gratified, especially when her campers rallied around her. Aimee even offered to beat up Nicole, an offer Elizabeth was almost tempted to accept. Then Lacey said she had given Nicole two weeks of kitchen duty—breakfast, lunch, dinner, and cleanup.

"It's the least she deserves," Lacey had said to a beaming Elizabeth.

But Maria hadn't approached her, and Elizabeth

blamed herself. *Maria will probably never forgive me for taking out my anger with Nicole on her,* Elizabeth wrote to Todd. Suddenly she felt someone walking up behind her. Elizabeth stopped writing and turned around.

It was Maria. "Elizabeth, can we talk?" she asked tentatively.

Elizabeth nodded, patting the ground beside her.

Maria plopped down and sighed, apparently gathering her thoughts.

Elizabeth held her breath, waiting with nervous anticipation to hear what Maria would say.

"I guess I'd better just start at the beginning," Maria said finally. "This last year was pretty tough. My parents moved us from Manhattan to the suburbs in the middle of the school year," she explained. "I was the new kid in a small town where it seemed like everyone had been friends since the first grade. They didn't need some new girl to join their cliques," Maria said sadly. "I was so lonely and desperate for friends, and Nicole was the only girl who was friendly to me. She kind of took me under her wing." Elizabeth couldn't imagine Nicole being friendly to anyone, but she kept silent, letting Maria talk.

"Now that I think about it, I should have known there was something wrong with Nicole. Besides me, she didn't have any other friends, and she'd gone to that school all her life." Maria paused and reached to the ground, picking up a rock. "I was just so grateful to have a friend, I guess I ignored the obvious." Maria threw the rock into the lake. "I can't believe what a fool I was," she said, her words catching in her throat.

Maria turned and looked at Elizabeth, her eyes full of tears. "I should have listened to you all along. Can you ever forgive me for not believing you?"

Elizabeth was so overcome with emotion that she couldn't speak. So she opened her arms and hugged Maria tightly.

Both girls sobbed, all the tension between them now gone.

With a rush Elizabeth started to feel more like herself than she had in days. *Finally the nightmare may be over,* she thought.

Elizabeth pulled back. "So, Maria," she said with a grin. "Did I hear you're in the market for a play to produce? Because I've got a little something I've been working on—it's called *Lakeside Love*."

Maria laughed. "I think I've heard of it," she said, her smile wide and happy.

"How does this outfit look?" Maria asked Elizabeth, spinning around to model her black embroidered vest worn over a filmy black skirt. Maria, Elizabeth, and Angela, the other JC from New York, were all in the cabin getting ready for the dance that night. Lila had gotten dressed early with Jessica to help her with last-minute details in the lodge, and Nicole was nowhere to be found.

Elizabeth's eyes widened as she looked Maria over. "You look absolutely fabulous," Elizabeth said. "Those three years in New York sure taught you something about putting an outfit together."

"It's nothing, really," Maria said. "Just wear a lot of black—that's what all the women in New York do."

"Well, it looks like I don't have much to choose from," Elizabeth said, eyeing her selection of brightly colored sundresses and skirts. Suddenly they all looked incredibly juvenile. She didn't want to look juvenile tonight. She was sick of feeling childish.

Maria walked over to look at Elizabeth's clothes. "Do you want to borrow something of mine?" she offered. "I think we're probably still about the same size."

Elizabeth chuckled. "Except that your legs are about twice as long as mine."

Maria looked down at her legs, then at Elizabeth's. "As long as we stick to miniskirts, we should be fine," Maria said, laughing. She shuffled through her things. She pulled out a black polo T-shirt dress. "How about this?"

Elizabeth bit her lip. She was in the mood for

something a little more exciting. "It's nice," she said noncommittally.

"A little too boring?" Maria asked.

"Well—"

Maria laughed. "It's okay. I think it's boring, too. But my mother just bought it for me and she would have been so hurt if I didn't bring it to camp." Maria smiled mischievously. "You know how mothers can be."

"Yes, I do," Elizabeth said with a laugh.

Maria pulled out a silver silk T-shirt and a tight black stretchy skirt. "How about this?"

Elizabeth shook her head. "That looks like something my sister would wear."

Maria looked at Elizabeth quizzically. "So what? Your sister's a great dresser," she said. "Besides, I think you would look sensational in this."

That stopped Elizabeth. Maria was right. Jessica was a great dresser, and if Jessica looked good in an outfit like that, so would Elizabeth. *So what if it's not what I'm used to wearing?* Elizabeth asked herself. *It's not like anyone here really knows the real me, anyway.* "Sure, why not?"

"Man, you look hot," Angela said after Elizabeth had finished dressing. "Who are you planning on seducing tonight?"

Elizabeth blushed. "I'm not planning on seducing anyone. I have a wonderful boyfriend back home," she said. Then the image of Joey's face

171

popped into Elizabeth's mind. She pushed it away. *I'm not wearing this for Joey Mason or for any other boy in camp. I love Todd,* she told herself.

Suddenly Angela shrieked.

Joey had popped his head in the door of the cabin. "Sorry to bother you girls, but is Nicole around?"

"Joey! You're not supposed to be here!" Maria scolded. "You're not even supposed to be on this side of the lake."

"I know, but I have to talk to Nicole," Joey said. "Do you know where she is?"

"No, I haven't seen her," Maria said coldly. "And I suggest you get out of here before Lacey catches you."

Joey put up his hands in a position of retreat. "OK, OK, I'm going. By the way," he said with a sexy grin. "You girls look great!"

Maria threw a pillow at him playfully. "You big flirt!"

Joey laughed and ran off, disappearing into the darkness.

Elizabeth finally let out the air she had sucked in when Joey first appeared. *Who am I kidding?* she asked herself. *I want to look sensational tonight for one reason and one reason only: Joey Mason.*

"Are you okay?" Maria asked. "You look a little pale."

"I'm fine," Elizabeth said. But as she fussed

with her hair, Elizabeth knew she wasn't fine. With everything that had happened today, Elizabeth should have been on cloud nine. But she wasn't. She couldn't stop thinking about watching Joey and Nicole together. The night would be torture.

"Are you ready to go?" Maria asked after a few minutes.

"Almost," Elizabeth said. "I just need my watch." She opened her nightstand drawer to get her watch, but the first thing she saw was her unfinished letter to Todd.

Elizabeth gulped. She hadn't sent Todd even one letter in over a week. Pretty soon he would start to wonder if something was wrong.

Well, something is wrong, she realized guiltily. *I'm infatuated with another guy.*

Jessica was filling the potato chip bowl when Elizabeth and Maria walked up to her.

"Jess! I've been looking for you," Elizabeth said.

"Well, you found me," Jessica said. Then she whistled. "Liz! You look incredibly hot!" she exclaimed. "Where did you get that outfit?"

Elizabeth blushed. "Maria lent it to me. Do you like it?"

"Like it? I *love* it. And you look great in it," Jessica said, impressed. *Elizabeth sure doesn't look like her boring self tonight,* she added silently. She looked at Maria. "You seem to be a good influence on my sister."

Maria laughed. "I hope so," she said, looking at Elizabeth with a sparkle in her eyes.

Jessica was glad to see the warmth between them—finally!

Maria gazed at the transformed lodge. "This place looks fabulous, Jessica! I'm really impressed."

"That's my sister," Elizabeth said proudly.

"Thanks, you guys. It does look pretty good, doesn't it?" Jessica looked around the room. She had to admit, the lodge looked magical.

"This is kind of fun to watch, isn't it?" Maria said. "The kids all look so cute."

Jessica surveyed the scene. The girls were busy giggling and pointing at the boys while the boys were busy acting as if they didn't notice. "They are cute," Jessica agreed.

Then Jessica spotted Nicole leading Joey out of the dance. She stole a glance at Elizabeth to see whether she had noticed. From the heartbroken look on Elizabeth's face, Jessica guessed that she'd seen them.

Buford and Johansen approached the girls. "Would you two like to dance?" they asked, looking at Elizabeth and Maria.

"Sure, I'll dance," Maria said cheerfully, leading Buford onto the dance floor.

Elizabeth frowned. "No thanks," she grumbled.

Johansen shuffled away, dejected.

"That wasn't very nice, Liz," Jessica said, surprised at Elizabeth's coldhearted behavior.

"Oh, so it's all right for Jessica Wakefield to reject guys right and left, but Elizabeth Wakefield has to be nice to everyone?" Elizabeth asked, her voice rising.

"No, I didn't mean that, it's just—"

Lila rushed up to Jessica, interrupting her midsentence. "Jess! You've got to shield me," she hissed, ducking behind Jessica. "Bo just walked into the dance."

"What, are you crazy? I'm not going to hide you all night," Jessica said, stepping away from Lila. "You're acting like a child. You're going to have to deal with Bo sooner or later." While they were setting up for the dance, Lila had finally explained to Jessica what had happened with Bo the night before.

"Why should I?" Lila asked rhetorically. "Why should I talk to him? He's just going to give some lame excuse about why he freaked out on me last night. But it all boils down to one thing: He rejected me. And if there's one thing I hate, it's rejection. I'm not about to take it from the same guy twice."

Jessica groaned. She sympathized with Lila, but she didn't want Lila hiding behind her all night. Jessica had suffered enough being constantly shadowed by the Wannabees over the past few days.

"Jess! He's coming! Hide me!" Lila squealed suddenly. Jessica looked up and noticed Bo striding across the room toward them.

"I'm not going to let you avoid him all night," Jessica proclaimed, stepping aside to reveal Lila.

"Well, I'm not going to stick around for this! If you need me, I'll be hiding out by the lake," Lila hissed. She raced off, running out the door.

"Lila! Wait!" Bo called after her. But she was gone.

Bo turned toward Jessica. "Do you know where she went?"

Jessica paused. Should she tell him? *Why not?* she decided. "Don't tell her I told you," Jessica said conspiratorially. "But you might try checking down by the lake."

"Thanks! I owe you one!" Bo said, running off in pursuit of Lila.

Jessica smiled. She couldn't quite figure out why, but she had a feeling Lila and Bo were made for each other.

"Lila! Where are you?" Bo called out. Lila was hiding under a flipped-over canoe, hoping Bo would just go away. "Lila? Lila? I know you're out here somewhere. Please come out!"

Never! Lila said to herself.

"Lila! Lila? C'mon! This isn't funny anymore," Bo said. His voice started quivering. "Lila! Please, Lila, I'm worried. I'm—" Then he started panting, his breath coming in short spurts. It sounded like he was hyperventilating.

Lila started to get worried. Bo wasn't calling out to her anymore. *What's wrong with him? What if he's being attacked by a bear?* Lila thought suddenly. She rushed out of her hiding place and saw Bo sitting on a rock, his head between his knees.

Lila ran over to Bo's slumped figure. "Bo! You're hyperventilating!" she exclaimed.

Still keeping his head lowered, Bo nodded silently.

Lila looked around the dark lake. There was no bear, nothing at all threatening that she could see. "What's wrong, Bo?" Lila asked, confused and concerned. "There's nothing here, nothing attacking you."

Finally Bo raised his head. "I'm a phony!" he wailed.

Lila took a step back. "What are you talking about?"

Bo took a few deep breaths. "Nobody calls me Bo," he confessed, shaking his head. "Nobody ever called me Bo."

Lila wrinkled her brow in confusion. "Then why—?" She paused.

"Why did I tell you Bo was my name?" Bo finished for her.

Lila nodded.

"Because I was ashamed of my real name:

Beauregard Creighton the Third," Bo said, his lips curling with disgust.

Lila was confounded. "Beauregard Creighton?" she asked, taking a step closer to Bo's seated figure. "The Third?"

Bo nodded silently. "It's OK, I can take it," he said. "You think it's the dopiest name you've ever heard."

"Well, it certainly is *different*," Lila conceded. But she wanted to know more. She sat down next to Bo on the rock. "Talk to me," she said earnestly. "Tell me who you are really."

Lila listened intently as Bo told her about his background. "My father, Beauregard Creighton Junior, is a self-made millionaire," Bo explained. "He was the hardworking son of a sharecropper who grew up to become president of a huge lobbying firm in Washington, D.C."

Bo frowned. "I don't expect you to understand this, but when your father has built his own fortune, everyone thinks that his son—me—is getting a free ride," Bo explained. "Which is probably the truth." Bo looked down in shame.

Lila was so shocked she couldn't speak.

"I'm a wimp, Lila," Bo continued. "I've never been rock climbing, never been kayaking, never been hang gliding. And I'm terrified of being alone in the dark," he explained. "That's why I didn't want to sneak to the girls' cabins last night." He buried his face in his hands in shame. "In fact, my father sent me to be a JC in the Montana wilderness to make me a man. But the truth is, I much prefer five-star hotels to tents. I've never been camping in my life."

Lila finally let out the breath she was holding during Bo's confession. Then she burst into laughter.

Bo looked up at Lila, hurt and humiliated. "You think I'm a total loser, don't you? Someone as brave as you probably can't even stand to be near someone as soft as me," he said dejectedly.

"No, no, wait," Lila said, trying to get her giggles under control. Then Lila explained her real self.

"You mean you didn't nearly die in Death Valley?" Bo asked when Lila had finished her confession.

Lila shook her head.

"And you come from one of the richest families in Sweet Valley, and your father's a self-made millionaire?"

Lila nodded.

Bo threw his arms around Lila.

I knew Bo was my destiny, Lila said to herself as she melted into his arms.

Then Bo pulled back from their embrace and looked seriously into Lila's eyes. "I need you to make me one promise, Lila Fowler," he said seriously.

"Anything," Lila whispered.

"Promise me you'll never make tree-bark tea again!" he said.

◦   ◦   ◦

A few yards away from where Bo and Lila sat staring soulfully into each other's eyes, Elizabeth was sitting on a rock, crying softly as she looked out at the water.

After her ugly behavior back at the dance, Elizabeth had decided she wasn't fit for human companionship. So she came out to the lake to be by herself.

Now she felt terrible for being so mean to Johansen and even worse for lashing out at Jessica, especially since she had only Jessica to thank for fixing her reputation. *First I lashed out at Maria, now Jessica. When will I start behaving like myself?* she wondered.

The first thing I've got to do is stop this crazy crush on Joey, Elizabeth decided. *And the best way to do that is to remind myself of all Todd's wonderful qualities and why I love him so much.* Elizabeth began the list in her mind. *He's kind, and he's cute, and he loves me, and . . .*

Elizabeth stopped. She had drawn a blank. She couldn't even picture Todd's face. With all her heart, Elizabeth wished she could remember her love for Todd. But Todd and her relationship with him seemed so far away, practically in another lifetime. *And in this lifetime I want to be with Joey,* Elizabeth thought.

Suddenly Joey stepped out of the darkness.

Elizabeth's heart stopped. *Am I hallucinating?*

she wondered. *Is my brain so scrambled that I'm seeing visions?*

But this vision started moving closer to Elizabeth. "Liz? Is that you?" Joey asked.

Startled, Elizabeth couldn't find her tongue to speak. So she nodded silently.

"Can I talk to you for a minute?" Joey asked, his voice soft and gentle.

Elizabeth found her voice. "Yes," she croaked.

Joey knelt down in front of Elizabeth and looked up into her eyes. "Let me start by saying how sorry I am for the things I've said to you," Joey said, taking her hand.

Elizabeth squeezed his fingers, feeling a rush of pleasure as she saw the way Joey's green eyes reflected the moonlight.

Joey continued. "It's not a good excuse, but I'd been caught in the web of Nicole's lies. And not only did she have me fooled, she had us all fooled." Then Joey explained how he'd been on the phone all afternoon with his connections on the East Coast. It turned out that Elizabeth's accusations had been right. Nicole had been suspected of plagiarism at nearly every theater where she'd worked. Nicole was just so good at covering her tracks that no one had been able to prove anything. Until Maggie's videotaped confession.

Elizabeth shook her head and smiled. "And we thought Maggie was just a nuisance."

Joey laughed. Then his face turned serious. "Now I realize that Nicole was out to ruin you. You *are* the special person I first thought you were from the moment I met you." Joey took a deep breath. "It's you I want, Elizabeth Wakefield. If you'll have me."

Elizabeth gulped. She opened her mouth to speak without even knowing which words would come out.

Joey raised a finger to her lips. "Before you say anything, first I have to ask you something. It's not my style to move in on another guy's girl, so I need to know what's up with this guy Todd. I've kind of been asking around, and from what everyone says, I get the feeling you're practically engaged."

Elizabeth gulped again, feeling guilty. But as she looked directly into Joey's eyes, she found herself shaking her head. "I don't know who told you that," she said. "It's really not serious between me and Todd. We're free to date other people." *What made me say that?* Elizabeth asked herself when she heard her own words echoing in her head.

Joey's face broke into a wide grin. "Boy, am I glad to hear that," he said.

Elizabeth smiled, but inside, her stomach was in knots. She had never lied so blatantly about her relationship with Todd. She knew she should tell Joey the truth. But when Elizabeth felt Joey moving in for a kiss, Elizabeth realized she was too intrigued to resist her feelings. She had yearned for the touch of his lips too much to stop them from touching her own lips now.

Their faces just inches apart, Elizabeth felt her heart throb. Suddenly there was a loud crash from the bushes behind them.

Joey jerked back. "What the—?" He jumped up and pulled the bushes apart.

"Hi, Joey," Tanya said. Sitting next to her was Maggie, with her video camera pointed directly at Elizabeth.

"You little devils! You should know better than to sneak up on people in the dark," Joey cried, sounding more amused than angry. Then he turned to Elizabeth. "We'd better make sure they get back to camp," he said, holding out a hand to help Elizabeth to her feet.

"But don't think you're off the hook, Ms. Wakefield," Joey whispered to Elizabeth as they followed the girls back to camp. "We'll continue this later. And that's a promise."

Chapter 12

"Jess! Are you still awake?" Lila whispered.

"Yes," Jessica grumbled.

"Did I tell you that Bo's mother goes to Paris twice a year for the spring and fall fashion shows? Can you imagine?"

"That's really great, Lila," Jessica replied. She wished Lila would shut up and just go to sleep already. "Aren't you getting tired?"

Lila rolled onto her back and looked out the window. "I'm too happy to sleep," she murmured dreamily.

Glancing over at Lila's wide-awake face, Jessica almost wished she hadn't sent Bo after Lila that evening. Jessica had to wait until everyone was asleep before she could sneak out to town to find Paul. And Lila wouldn't stop gushing about Bo and his rich, influential family.

Jessica hadn't even confided to Lila what she was planning to do. She knew she was taking a huge risk, and she had no idea what the payoff would be. Lila would certainly have tried to talk Jessica out of it, and Jessica didn't want to be talked out of it. The thrill of her upcoming adventure was too attractive. And so was Paul.

Finally she heard Lila's dainty little telltale snore. Jessica smiled, thinking about how Lila always refused to believe it when Jessica told her she snored. *Even royalty snores, Lila Fowler,* she said to herself.

Still dressed in her party outfit under her pajamas, Jessica crept out of the cabin. She couldn't use a flashlight for fear of drawing attention. But the moon was bright enough to light Jessica's way to where Lacey kept her Bronco parked out back behind the main lodge.

Good thing it slipped Lacey's mind to ask for these back, Jessica thought as she pulled the car keys out of her pocket. Luckily the Bronco was parked on a slight incline, so Jessica didn't turn on the motor right away. She released the parking brake and shifted into neutral. Once the truck had rolled away from the building, Jessica turned the ignition key. The motor hummed to life.

Jessica drove with the headlights off until she was out on the two-lane highway. Then she flipped on the lights and sped into town.

By the time she got there, it was after one in the morning. The town looked dead. *There's no way I'll be able to find Paul,* Jessica worried. *But I can't turn back without trying.* Then Jessica spotted an unlit neon sign with the words MATTIE'S DINER. *This is it!* Jessica said to herself as she pulled into the parking lot.

She spotted Paul taking the trash out to the dumpsters at the side of the building. *He's here!* Jessica thought with excitement, clutching the steering wheel tightly with sweaty palms.

Paul squinted against the headlights of the Bronco. "We're closed!" he shouted after Jessica parked and cut the engine.

Jessica opened the car door and jumped out. "I know," she said. "I didn't come for the food."

Paul opened his mouth in surprise. "It's you!"

Jessica was glad to see that he looked flustered. But then his expression turned angry.

"What are you doing here in the middle of the night?" he yelled. "You're not supposed to leave camp!"

Jessica frowned, hurt by his less than enthusiastic reception. "It's good to see you, too," she replied sarcastically.

Paul tossed the garbage bags he was carrying onto the ground. "First you dye my little sister's hair blond, then you totally disobey the rules and leave camp in the middle of the night? Every single parent who sent their kids to that camp can only sleep at night thinking there are responsible, mature counselors looking after their children. What kind of counselor are you?" Paul raged.

Jessica got defensive. "I'm a great counselor— the best junior counselor in the camp," she said defensively. "Lacey says so herself."

Paul looked at the Bronco. "Did Lacey say you could drive her truck or did you steal it?"

"I didn't steal it! She gave me her keys!"

"To drive into town in the middle of the night? What did you come here for, anyway?"

"Whatever I came for, it's none of your business!" Jessica shouted. She jumped into the Bronco and peeled out of the parking lot.

Paul's the biggest jerk I've ever met in my life! Jessica thought as she drove off. *I risked everything I've worked for this week to see him. All for nothing. How could I have been so stupid?*

Tanya, that's how, she remembered. Tanya had told her Paul couldn't stop asking questions about Jessica. Had her camper made the whole thing up to humiliate her? Was Tanya not the adoring member of the Jessica Wakefield fan club that she made herself out to be? *I'm going to have to have a little talk with that girl,* Jessica thought grimly.

Halfway back to camp the Bronco suddenly bobbed and swerved. One of the tires had blown! Jessica held fast to the steering wheel and gently braked, pulling over to the side of the road.

She cut the engine and listened to the silence. Luckily she had some experience changing flats. But she'd never had to do it on a deserted mountain road in the middle of the night.

Jessica took a deep breath and got out of the Bronco. She went to the back and opened the compartment that held the spare tire.

It was empty.

A huge wave rocked the tiny sailboat, sending Elizabeth crashing over the slippery deck. She clung to the railing, holding on for dear life as her legs dangled down into the water below.

Elizabeth heard a voice from above. "Grab my hand!" Elizabeth looked up and saw Todd's face hanging over the deck. He was reaching an arm down to her. "Grab my hand!" he yelled again.

Elizabeth loosened the fingers of her left hand, summoning the courage to reach out to Todd. Then the boat suddenly jerked, hit by another wave. Elizabeth screamed, clutching the railing tighter. "I can't let go!" Elizabeth cried.

"I'll save you!" said a voice from below. Elizabeth looked down and saw Joey rowing up next to her in a lifeboat.

"Climb up to me!" Todd cried from above.

"Jump down to me!" Joey cried from below.

Clinging to the boat's flimsy railing, Elizabeth

was frozen with indecision. What should she do?

Then she heard some sort of scratching noise. It didn't go away.

Elizabeth woke up with a jolt, realizing that although the dream wasn't real, the noise was. Somebody was scratching on the window screen above the foot of her bed. Elizabeth sat up and rubbed her eyes. Looking out the window, she saw Joey, beckoning for her to come outside.

Elizabeth glanced at the unopened letter from Todd that was sitting on her nightstand and the memory of her dream washed over her. *What did it mean?* Elizabeth wondered. *It didn't tell me anything. It just made my dilemma crystal clear.*

Elizabeth peeked out the window again and saw Joey waiting expectantly for her. *I can't just let him stand there,* Elizabeth thought. Just like Todd, Joey was an innocent in the whole affair. If Elizabeth didn't go meet him, he might think he had done something wrong. And he hadn't. Only she had.

Elizabeth jumped out of bed and tiptoed through the dark cabin toward the door, trying to avoid the squeakiest of the floorboards. Passing by Jessica's bed, Elizabeth was surprised to see that although the bedsheets were rumpled, Jessica wasn't in it. *Where's Jessica?* she wondered.

Distracted by her sister's disappearance, Elizabeth stubbed her toe on something. It was

Nicole's bed! *Just my luck!* Elizabeth cursed, forgetting about her missing twin. She held her breath as Nicole stirred in her sleep. Then Nicole lay still. Elizabeth smiled. *If you only knew where I'm sneaking off to right now, you'd eat your sheets,* Elizabeth thought nastily as she continued out of the cabin.

Joey stood in the light of the moon. "These are for you," he whispered, pulling a bouquet of wildflowers from behind his back.

"Thank you, Joey," Elizabeth whispered, cradling the bouquet in her arms. "You sneaked all the way over here just to give me these?"

"No, that's not the only reason," Joey said mysteriously. He took Elizabeth by the hand and led her toward the lake.

Elizabeth followed silently, terrified about what she was doing yet unable to stop herself.

Down by the dock Joey stopped and faced Elizabeth. He looked down at her, cupping her face in his hands. "Now, let's finish what we started," he said huskily. Then he enveloped Elizabeth in a passionate kiss.

Elizabeth swooned, feeling dizzy with desire.

To make sure she wasn't still dreaming, Elizabeth opened her eyes. Over Joey's shoulder Elizabeth spotted a figure standing by the shore. It was Nicole. Even in the dark Elizabeth could see the look of fury on Nicole's face. *I guess I woke her up after all*, Elizabeth realized. *Serves her right.*

Elizabeth threw her arms even tighter around Joey, kissing him with a fervor that was part desire for the gorgeous guy in her arms and part delicious, thrilling revenge.

Score another round for Elizabeth Wakefield, she thought triumphantly.

Jessica was still sitting in the driver's seat, fretting over what to do, when she heard a car coming from the direction of the town. *I'm saved!* she thought immediately, turning on her hazard lights.

Then Jessica was struck by a horrible thought. *What if it's some crazed lunatic or even the phantom woodsman? I could be murdered and chopped up in a thousand pieces,* she fretted. *Or worse—it could be Lacey!*

Jessica held her breath, full of hope and terror as she watched the headlights get closer in her rearview mirror. The car pulled up behind her and the driver's-side door opened. Jessica's heart pounded in her chest as she saw a man step out. Then her heart skipped a beat. It was Paul!

"I see you didn't get too far," Paul joked as he ambled up to her open window.

Jessica's relief turned to anger. "If you're going to just stand there and humiliate me, I suggest you leave right now," she said.

Paul reached into the window and caressed

Jessica's cheek. "I'm sorry, that was very insensitive of me," he said gently. "You must be terrified, getting a flat tire on a strange deserted road in the middle of the night."

Jessica looked at Paul's concerned expression. *Is this the same Paul who just screamed at me in the parking lot?* she wondered. "I did get pretty scared," she admitted.

"Well, I'm glad I decided to come after you," Paul said.

Jessica looked at him in surprise.

"After you tore out of town, it suddenly hit me what a fool I was to rip into you like that. You sneaked into town to see me, didn't you?"

Jessica nodded.

"My blabbermouth sister Tanya must have spilled the beans about how I'd been asking about you," Paul said.

Jessica nodded again.

Paul reached out a hand and touched Jessica's chin, lifting her face to look straight into her eyes. "I can be pretty stupid sometimes," he said. "Please forgive me?"

Jessica felt herself drowning in Paul's deep, dark eyes. "I'll think about it," she said after a moment. "After you fix my flat tire." She flashed him a flirtatious smile.

"No sweat!" Paul replied enthusiastically. Jessica jumped out of the Bronco and watched as

Paul deftly jacked up the truck and unfastened the guilty tire. Then he retrieved a brand-new tire that was in the back of his truck.

"How can I ever thank you?" Jessica asked after Paul had finished.

"You can start by letting me kiss those devastating lips of yours," Paul said. He put one arm around her shoulders and pulled her in for a heart-stopping kiss. His slightly sweaty, slightly greasy scent from working in the restaurant made Jessica's nose tingle wonderfully.

"Better get back to camp, little girl," Paul said after a minute of sensational kisses. "You wouldn't want the bogeyman to get you."

They kissed once more, and then Jessica climbed into Lacey's Bronco and drove away.

Even if I get caught, it was worth it, Jessica thought as she made her way toward the camp, feeling faint with bliss.

Chapter 13

"I needed this break. The sun feels so good," Elizabeth said, stretching her arms above her head. After a successful first read-through of Elizabeth's play that afternoon in workshop, Joey and Elizabeth had taken a swim out to the wooden dock in the middle of the lake. Now they lay drying in the sun.

"Are you sure it's not too strong? The sun can be pretty brutal up here in the mountains, and I wouldn't want you to burn yourself," Joey said with concern. "It's not like that bikini provides much coverage."

Elizabeth laughed. "My body will be fine," she said flirtatiously.

Joey chuckled. "I'll say," he said appreciatively.

Elizabeth usually didn't wear such revealing

swimwear, but when Joey asked her to go sun-bathing, she wanted to look fantastic. Since she hadn't packed any fantastic bathing suits, she took the liberty of borrowing Jessica's sexy new green bikini. *Jessica won't mind,* Elizabeth had reasoned when she went into her twin's dresser without asking. *After all, she's borrowed clothing of mine a million times without asking. Plus, she owes me one—for keeping my mouth shut about her sneaking off into town.*

The night before, Joey and Elizabeth had nearly collided with Jessica in the dark as they were walking back to the JC cabin from the lake.

"I was in the bathroom," Jessica had explained quickly.

Elizabeth had let it go, not wanting to make a scene in front of Joey.

But this morning after the flag-raising cere-mony Elizabeth confronted Jessica, demanding the truth. When Jessica fessed up, Elizabeth was initially hurt and angry that Jessica had sneaked out without even telling her. Then she got over it. After all, Jessica was fine, the Bronco was fine, and Lacey was none the wiser. And Jessica was clearly ecstatic about this Paul guy. Why should Elizabeth get in the way of Jessica's new passion?

Isn't love grand? Elizabeth mused to herself, enjoying the way the afternoon sun gently soothed her body. She felt happier than she had in days. In a matter of twenty-four hours Elizabeth's situation had made a complete turnaround. Nicole was ruined, Elizabeth's friendship with Maria was fixed, her play was being produced, and Lacey seemed to be warming up to her. Even Elizabeth's campers had been relatively well behaved that morning at breakfast.

Suddenly Elizabeth felt a cold trickle on her belly. She squinted her eyes open and saw Joey cupping a handful of lake water over her body. "Hey! What do you think you're doing?" Elizabeth demanded, a smile on her face.

"Just cooling you down," Joey said. Then he dumped his whole handful of water.

Elizabeth jerked up, shocked by the blast of cold. "I'll get you!" she said. And she shoved Joey off the dock into the lake.

"Hey!" Joey cried when he came up for air.

"Race you back to shore!" Elizabeth called out to him from the dock.

"You're on!" Joey turned and started a brisk stroke toward the shore.

"No fair, you're taking a head start!" Elizabeth cried.

"So catch up with me!" Joey called back to her.

Elizabeth took a running start from the dock and sprang into the lake, breaking out into a powerful stroke when she surfaced from her dive.

They made it to shore at exactly the same time.

"You're a pretty impressive swimmer," Joey said, taking Elizabeth's hand as they climbed out of the lake and walked through the woods back to camp.

"Thanks to having a pool in my backyard and an ocean in my front yard," Elizabeth replied.

"Ahh, the life. You southern Californians have it so easy," Joey said. "Manhattan may be surrounded by water, but no one in their right mind swims in the Hudson or the East River."

Elizabeth and Joey were still laughing and holding hands when they rounded the corner of the main lodge.

Then Elizabeth stopped short. Parked next to the lodge was a black BMW.

"What's wrong?" Joey asked.

But Elizabeth couldn't speak. Todd was standing next to his car, and he seemed to be having an intense conversation with Nicole.

Then he looked up and spotted Elizabeth and Joey. "Elizabeth," Todd called across the lot. "We need to talk."

Elizabeth dropped Joey's hand. *This can't be happening,* she thought.

SWEET VALLEY HIGH™

Bantam Books in the Sweet Valley High series. Ask your bookseller for the books you have missed.

SWEET VALLEY HIGH™

THRILLER EDITIONS

MURDER ON THE LINE
MURDER IN PARADISE

SWEET VALLEY HIGH SUPER STARS

BRUCE'S STORY
ENID'S STORY
TODD'S STORY

SUPER EDITIONS
SPECIAL CHRISTMAS
PERFECT SUMMER
SPRING FEVER

SPECIAL EDITIONS
THE WAKEFIELDS OF SWEET VALLEY
THE WAKEFIELD LEGACY

created by Francine Pascal

The *valley* has never been so *sweet*!

Having left Sweet Valley High School behind them, Jessica and Elizabeth Wakefield have begun a new stage in their lives, attending the most popular university around – Sweet Valley University!

Join them and all their friends for fun, frolics and frights on *and* off campus. How can you resist not too?

Ask your bookseller for any titles you may have missed. The Sweet Valley University series is published by Bantam Books.